Praise for *Don't Vote for Me*

"David's narrative is a blend of candor and wry humor, conveying his earnestness beneath his uncertainty and bluster. His growing understanding of Veronica's struggle to achieve her dreams in music and life contributes to his increasing ambivalence about the election. Ultimately, David's emerging maturity is honestly won and will resonate with readers. A comic romp that's also an enlightening quest for increased awareness and self-understanding."

—*Kirkus Reviews*

"Written in first-person narrative with lively similes, this is a fast-paced, humorous, and engaging story. Through the use of situational irony and inferences, misconceptions are overturned, leading the characters to learn valuable lessons."

—*School Library Connection*

Van Dolzer…keeps the tone light between David's wry observations, amusing friends, and the goofy predicaments he falls into.

—*Publishers Weekly*

Genuinely sweet...readers looking for realistic middle-grade fiction will find David a likable guide in a balanced lesson about ceding the spotlight.

—*School Library Journal*

A refreshing look at the importance of challenging one another to do our best no matter the circumstance, this book dares each of us to take risks and make the most of every opportunity, no matter how daunting it may seem.

—*Middle Shelf Magazine*

DON'T VOTE FOR ME

KRISTA VAN DOLZER

sourcebooks
jabberwocky

Published by Sourcebooks Jabberwocky, an imprint of Sourcebooks, Inc.
P.O. Box 4410, Naperville, Illinois 60567-4410
(630) 961-3900
Fax: (630) 961-2168
www.sourcebooks.com

The Library of Congress has cataloged the hardcover edition as follows:

Van Dolzer, Krista.
  Don't vote for me / Krista Van Dolzer.
    pages cm
  Summary: Roped into running for class president against the most popular girl in school, sixth-grader David discovers another side to his opponent when they are also paired up for the spring musical recital.
  (13 : alk. paper) [1. Elections--Fiction. 2. Popularity--Fiction. 3. Middle schools--Fiction. 4. Schools--Fiction.] I. Title. II. Title: Do not vote for me.
  PZ7.V2737Do 2015
  [Fic]--dc23
                          2014046574

Source of Production: Versa Press, East Peoria, Illinois, USA
Date of Production: May 2016
Run Number: 5006716

       Printed and bound in the United States of America.
               VP 10 9 8 7 6 5 4 3 2

For Kate,
who never quit

ONE

THERE WERE THREE KINDS of kids at Shepherd's Vale Middle School: the populars, the unpopulars, and Riley and me. It wasn't that we were disliked; it was that we were invisible. We could have dressed up like Martian pirates—the costumes were two Halloweens old, but we hadn't grown much—and no one would have noticed.

So when I saw that sign-up sheet, I didn't stop to think about what I was going to say, just caught Riley's eye and flicked a thumb over my shoulder. "Looks like it's time for the Pritchard-Pratt's annual coronation."

This year's sign-up sheet was especially optimistic: *ARE YOU THE NEXT CLASS PRESIDENT?* it asked in big, exciting letters. Unless your name was Veronica Pritchard-Pratt, my guess was probably not. Still, it encouraged you to *SIGN UP BY MAY 2ND!*

Veronica's name was the only one on the list.

Riley dragged a hand under his nose. "I don't know

why they bother." His nose ran all the time, but when he came into contact with mice, ragweed, or populars, it ran even worse. "Might as well save the tree."

Not that my man Riley believed in saving trees. He was an actual writer, so he spent more time writing stories than he spent playing Batman and sleeping *combined.* He scribbled them down in his notebook, and no one—and I mean, *no one*—was allowed to come near it.

I turned my thumb toward my chest. "They bother because they know I come from a long line of litigators, so they know I'd sue their butts off if they tried anything funny!"

My parents were the litigators (well, *former* litigators, which was the fancy way of saying they used to sue their clients' competitors for sneezing in their presence), and the truth was, they'd be appalled if they knew I was threatening to take someone to court. Riley didn't seem thrilled, either. He glanced nervously around the commons, but Ms. Quintero, the principal, was nowhere in sight.

"But what they don't know," I went on, "is that making false claims is also grounds for a lawsuit. Do they really think we're dumb enough to think we could win? The Pritchard-Pratt hasn't lost a race in the last three years."

I'd dug terms like "false claims" and "grounds" out of Mom and Dad's old law books. I liked the way they made me sound like I knew what I was talking about.

"But why should we have to settle for the Pritchard-Pratt?" I demanded. "Does she represent our views, our opinions?"

The words poured out of me like water from a backed-up toilet. I'd been gaining volume, and now most of the kids scattered around the commons were staring up—or down—at me. Their attention made me want to keep talking, talking, talking.

"No!" I said, raising my fist. "So I say it's time we fight!"

Stronger words hadn't been spoken since that Patrick Henry guy had said, *Give me liberty, or give me death!* The other kids responded by raising their fists, too, and whispering urgently to their neighbors. Hope bloomed in my chest like a helium balloon. For the first time in my life, someone was paying attention.

At least my man Riley kept my feet on the ground. "You talk too much," he mumbled.

"Maybe you don't talk enough."

It was clearly a challenge, but he didn't take the bait. "Let's get out of here," he said instead, brushing his hair into his eyes. When it came time for fight or flight, Riley always chose the latter.

I probably would have stayed, but Riley had been my best bro since my real bros had moved out, so I couldn't ditch him. Besides, I'd said my piece. They could take it or leave it (and judging the future by the past, I could guess which one they'd pick).

But I would guess wrong.

By the start of second period, the whispers from the commons had taken over the band room, and they were getting louder. The other band geeks, or BGs, nudged me as they passed or caught my eye and winked. I tried to play it cool—I'd never realized how awkward it could get when people noticed you—and I could have pulled it off if it hadn't been for *her*.

I was already in my seat, warming up my mouthpiece, when Veronica appeared. She didn't come in right away, just stood outside the door while Hector and Samantha did their usual sweep. They acted like the Secret Service on the prowl for glitter bombs. The other, lesser populars, whose names I'd never learned, lingered in the hall and tried not to breathe our air.

Once Hector and Samantha deemed the room fit for her presence, Veronica nodded to her sidekicks, then pecked Brady on the lips.

It was only a peck, but I still looked away. Why they were the populars while Riley and I were barely clinging to the sixth grade's social ladder's lowest rungs, I couldn't have said. They should have been absent more often, since they seemed so fond of swapping bacteria.

As soon as she stepped through the door, the whispers died down to a hum. The other BGs were obviously waiting for a shoot-out (or maybe a plastic lightsaber duel), but I had no interest in being a floor show. I pretended not to notice, but as the moments stretched to seconds, then to almost a minute, I couldn't help but sneak a peek. At least Brady and the Terrible Twins had finally wandered off. She was pulling her music out of her bright-green messenger, which looked as out of place in the band room as my bulky black backpack would have looked at a student council meeting.

I tried to focus on *my* music as she picked her way through the BGs, who were scurrying around her ankles like busy worker ants. That was a slight exaggeration—they might have come up to her waist—but she *was* a giantess. Rumor had it that her dad had played for the Utah Jazz back when they were good, but since YouTube hadn't been around in the Stone Age, no one could confirm it.

No sooner had she reached the risers than I lowered my gaze. If she thought I'd been staring, I might die of shame. I tried to practice my buzzing, but when I caught a whiff of watermelon, I couldn't help but draw a deep breath.

The piano was right next to the trumpets, so I couldn't ignore her without looking like I was trying to ignore her. "You made my mouth water," I said, then realized how that must have sounded. "I mean, your perfume made my mouth water. Because it smells like watermelon." I shook my head. "I'm gonna stop talking now."

"You should have done that sooner."

The bell spared me the embarrassment of sticking my other foot in my mouth. I said a silent prayer to the bell gods—they probably didn't get very many—as Mr. Ashton, our teacher, finally breezed into the room.

Mr. Ashton took more bathroom breaks than Granny Grainger, and he was always the last teacher to roll into the parking lot on Monday mornings. But he had a degree in choral conducting and a diploma from Lietz House, the most prestigious music magnet in the greater Salt Lake area, so Ms. Quintero had no choice but to put up with his quirks.

"Good morning!" Mr. Ashton boomed. His voice shook the ceiling tiles. "We'll pick up right where we left off—with 'The Stars and Stripes Forever'!"

I attached my mouthpiece to my trumpet, but before I could take a breath, a voice behind me growled, "Quit acting like you think you're friends."

I glanced over my shoulder. "*Excuse me?*"

Mr. Ashton rapped his music stand with his crooked baton (which was actually the wand he'd bought on his last trip to Orlando, but if you tried to call it that, he would poke you in the stomach and deduct ten points from Slytherin). "David, your attention!"

Scowling, I raised my trumpet. Mr. Ashton thumped out four beats so we could find our rhythm, but just before the music swelled, the voice behind me hissed, "You said she was the enemy."

The air rushed out of my lungs, forcing a squeal out of my trumpet, but the other squeals and squeaks covered up my ugly note. I glanced over my shoulder again, trying to catch a glimpse of whoever the voice belonged to, but everyone looked guilty. When you had to blow into a mouthpiece to butcher a classic, you couldn't help but get red-faced.

As I twisted around, I managed to force out a B flat that only sounded slightly sharp, but that wasn't what made me wince. Though Veronica had been playing a few seconds ago, she wasn't playing now. She was staring straight ahead, her fingers frozen on the keys. She could have been lost inside the melody, but somehow, I knew she wasn't.

Somehow, I knew she'd heard.

Guilt wriggled in my stomach like a ball of unchewed worms—I hadn't even wondered what she might think of my rant—but before I had a chance to do something about it, Mr. Ashton waved us off.

"No, no!" he said angrily as he bashed his music stand. "'The Stars and Stripes Forever' needs more life, more oomph, than that! Let's take it from the top, and this time, try to emote!"

I was more concerned about the voice than these stupid stars and stripes, and as it turned out, I had a reason to be. While Mr. Ashton rearranged his music, the voice behind me asked, "What do you say, Grainger? Are you gonna take her on?"

The guilt was so strong that I leaped out of my seat. "That's it!" I said indignantly. "If you have something to say to me, then say it to my face!"

"The Stars and Stripes Forever" cut off with one last wheeze from the tubas. It was like a giant spotlight was suddenly shining down on me, glinting off my uncombed hair and the angry purple pimple I'd discovered on my nose that morning. I felt my cheeks get hot, but I didn't sit down. That would only make it worse.

Mr. Ashton cleared his throat. "David, a word," he said so softly that the ceiling tiles didn't tremble.

I drew a nervous breath, then set my trumpet back down. I couldn't look at Veronica. I couldn't look at anyone.

Mr. Ashton marched into the hall, and I had no choice but to follow. As soon as I caught up, he pulled the door shut on my heels. I stared at the industrial-grade carpet, and Mr. Ashton stared at me. We stared for a long time.

"Believe it or not," he finally said, "I think I understand you." He folded his arms across his chest. "And I know just what you need."

I glanced up at him. "You do?" Mom had already tried several dozen interventions, but so far, they hadn't worked.

Mr. Ashton nodded knowingly. "You've got a restless spirit, David—a sensitive muse, if you will. I suspect that crushing it will only lead to more flare-ups." He pretended to tie a knot with an imaginary rope. "We need to harness it instead."

I didn't like the way that he'd tied that knot. It made me think of a noose. "Thanks, Mr. Ashton," I replied as I tugged at my collar. Was it my imagination, or did it suddenly seem tighter? "But if it's all the same to you, I think I'd rather forget it. I've never been much of a spirit harnesser."

He opened his mouth to answer, but I held up my hands.

"I know what you're gonna say," I said, "and I'm sorry for wigging out. It won't happen again. Well, I guess it might happen again, but I'll do my very best."

I reached behind my back and tried to grab hold of the handle, but Mr. Ashton wasn't done. Either he was very bad at interpreting social cues, or he was very good at listening to himself talk.

"I appreciate that promise, but I meant what I said. I want to help you, David, and I really think I can."

"Okay, Mr. Ashton." I'd discovered that the quickest way to get rid of a pest was to agree with him. "But if it's all the same to you, I'd like to go back in now."

This time, I didn't wait for him to cut off my escape, just grabbed hold of the handle and pushed open the door. If Mr. Ashton *was* like me, he'd get sick of this idea within a day or two. I just had to wait him out.

TWO

BY THE TIME LUNCH rolled around, everyone in the sixth grade had heard about my little speech (not to mention my meltdown). When I walked into the lunchroom, conversation suddenly ceased. Eyes zipped back and forth between Veronica and me, but it didn't look like she'd noticed. She was eating her usual bagel while she pretended to be riveted by the dark-haired popular who was sitting beside her. They were the only two people who hadn't reacted.

I tightened my grip on my lunch box and waited for her to turn around, but she just sat there listening. Maybe the dark-haired popular really was riveting, or maybe she was just going out of her way to ignore me completely. It dawned on the other kids that she wasn't going to make a scene at the same time it dawned on me. A deep breath whooshed out of the room (or maybe that was just my lungs), and everyone went back to whatever they'd been doing.

I hadn't been doing anything, so I plopped down on the bench across from Riley and Spencer (who still hadn't moved a muscle). Though Riley and I had been best bros for as long as we could talk, Spencer hadn't joined our group until the start of the third grade. His family had just moved to Shepherd's Vale (or SV, as I called it), so he hadn't had time to make any new friends. Our teacher had assigned us to sit with him at lunch, and after getting us to laugh by squirting milk out of his nose, then letting it drip back into the carton so he could squirt it out again, Spencer had become the third in our unfinished quartet.

But he wasn't laughing now. Neither was Riley. I pretended not to notice as I unpacked my lunch. Most kids didn't think that lunch boxes were cool anymore, but I strongly disagreed. I'd collected them since preschool, and though I only had a few, the Tick's was my favorite. He wasn't the fiercest-looking dude, but since he could get away with wearing spandex without getting beat up, I figured he was worth admiring.

I managed to unwrap my sandwich—PB and bananas, my favorite—before either of them could get a word out. "Did you come here to sit, or did you come here to eat?"

At least that snapped them out of it. "You know

they know," Spencer said, revealing a wad of partially chewed French fry.

I decided to play dumb at the last second. "Know *what*?" I replied.

Spencer stuck his chin out. "What you said about Veronica."

I scrambled to come up with an answer that didn't make me look like an idiot, but that answer didn't exist. "I guess I don't know what you mean."

"I was there, too," Riley mumbled, "so don't even try to lie to us."

"Yeah," Spencer replied. "I got the scoop from Arthur Dibbs, and you know if Arthur knows, then the whole school knows, too." He massaged one of his temples with the end of a French fry. "For Newton's sake, what were you thinking?"

Spencer wasn't scientific, but he didn't want his parents, who'd gotten degrees in biochemistry from one of those Ivy League schools, to think he was a dumbhead, so he Googled famous scientists and threw their names around like he'd heard of them before. The only problem was, he hadn't.

"I don't remember," I replied, taking a bite of my sandwich. "I wasn't thinking, just…talking."

Riley made a face. "And look where *that* got you."

I chucked my sandwich back into my lunch box. I wasn't hungry anymore. "So I whined about the Pritchard-Pratt. I whine about *everyone*."

Spencer smacked his forehead. "You can't whine about Veronica. She's Veronica, for Pasteur's sake! Do you have any idea what kinds of repercussions this will have on the greater geek community?"

I arched an eyebrow. "Repercussions?"

"You know, bad stuff," Riley said.

I rolled my eyes. "I *know*."

"Do you?" Spencer asked, aiming a French fry at my chest. "Or have you already forgotten Arthur's horrible dance-off?"

"Of course I haven't," I replied, and for once, it was true. Everyone remembered Arthur's dance-off (but that wasn't necessarily a good thing). No sooner had he challenged Brady to a duel than Brady had busted a sweet move and knocked Arthur off his feet. He'd literally fallen on his face and broken his nose in three places, and that was just a dancing duel. This was ten thousand times more serious.

Spencer motioned toward the populars. "You've got to fix this, David. You've got to go over there and tell her you didn't really mean it."

"But what if I *did* mean it?" I asked.

"You didn't," they replied.

Still, I wasn't convinced. I hadn't meant to take potshots at Veronica, but words had to come from somewhere. And the thought of walking over there, of mumbling, "I'm sorry," while the other populars looked on, was almost more than I could bear. When I glanced over my shoulder, I saw that Hector was dismantling the remnants of his chicken wing, tearing off strips of meat with methodical precision. Meanwhile, Samantha was massaging each of her knuckles in turn and shooting threatening looks my way. I had zero doubt that they were going to kill me.

Hector and Samantha were the most brutal kids in the sixth grade (and had been for some time). They'd long since mastered wedgies—in fact, they'd probably invented them—and rumor had it that Samantha had spent most of winter break studying ancient bamboo torture in some temple in Shanghai. Also, Hector and Samantha swore like late-night cartoon characters. Riley thought they swore because their vocabularies wouldn't fill the front and back of a Post-it Note, but I thought they swore because they were the populars, and as we all knew, populars could get away with anything.

But I refused to let them get away with me.

"No," I finally said. "I'm not gonna apologize."

Spencer smacked his forehead again. We kept telling him he'd lose brain cells if he kept smacking his forehead, but so far, that hadn't stopped him. "What are you, insane?"

"No," Riley said darkly, "he's just suicidal."

"I'm not suicidal," I said, flicking one of Spencer's French fries at him. "And I'm not insane, either. I just don't think we should have to bow down to these bozos." Or at least I'd thought that this morning. "I mean, who died and made them popular?"

"We did," Spencer said. "We talk about what clothes they wear, what songs they listen to, and what movies and TV shows they watch. They're popular because we say they are, but do they ever repay us?" He stuffed a French fry in his mouth. "Don't they know that all we want is a seat on student council?"

"I don't," Riley said.

"Me neither," I admitted.

Spencer's eyes bulged. "*What?* I'd swear off trans fats for a year if someone would give me a seat!"

I flicked a thumb over my shoulder. "Well, you're never gonna get one if Veronica keeps deciding. She doesn't even know your name."

Two of the many perks of winning the popularity contest that we called an election were getting to fill the five-seat student council and getting to pick a vice, who, along with the class president, ran the student council meetings and coordinated with Ms. Quintero on "important school business" (according to the school constitution). Whoever had come up with this idea clearly wasn't a BG. We'd been underrepresented since 1787.

Spencer opened his mouth to answer, but before he could get a word out, his attention shifted to something—or someone—over my shoulder. Grudgingly, I turned around. Veronica was climbing onto the populars' table, giving everyone a look at her signature All Stars. They were in such good condition that they looked brand-new, but I'd been shopping secondhand since Radcliff, one of my brothers, had introduced me to the art nearly six years earlier. Those skinnier toe caps meant that that pair of All Stars was thirty years old (at least). If Radcliff had been here, he probably would have offered her his whole PEZ collection—not to mention his firstborn child—for those vintage shoes.

I tried to tell myself that her plans had nothing to do with me, but I still wanted to dash. Except I couldn't move. Not even the lunch ladies were immune to Veronica's powers. One of them tried to intervene, but one look from Veronica froze the woman in her tracks.

Veronica surveyed the lunchroom like a queen surveying her kingdom. "It has come to my attention that a certain unnamed someone thinks I don't have the perspective to speak for this class. Now, I'll remind this someone that I've won the last two elections without breaking a sweat, but in case *you* think I won because no one ran against me, let me set the record straight. I'm perfectly willing to campaign against anyone—and I mean, *anyone*—who thinks he or she can beat me." She scanned the crowd with frosty eyes—until those eyes landed on me. "So by all means, join the race. And may the best candidate win."

She held my gaze for one more second, then tossed her hair over her shoulder and hopped down from the table. Brady extended his hand, but she paid it no heed. After disposing of her bagel, she swept out of the lunchroom with her nose in the air.

While her friends raced to catch up, I just sat there, stunned. I'd already lost my appetite, but now I was afraid that I might lose my lunch. I wrapped an arm around my stomach and hunkered down behind my lunch box. Maybe if I asked him nicely, the Tick would fight my battles for me.

Riley shivered from head to toes. "What are you going to do?" he whispered.

"What do you think?" I asked. "I'm gonna hightail it to Panama and open up a taco shop."

"You can't make tacos," he said. "And I don't think they eat them there, anyway."

"And," Spencer replied, "you don't have a passport. I'd let you borrow mine, but you're pastier than I am."

Spencer was the only kid in SV who had an actual passport, which he used to travel between SV and Hong Kong. He was born in New Hampshire (or maybe New Jersey), but his parents were Hong Kongans (or whatever you called them).

I knotted my arms across my chest. "Then I'll just do nothing," I said.

Spencer rolled his eyes. "You can't do nothing," he replied. "That's what we've been trying to tell you."

"Of course I can," I replied, coating each word with confidence. "I'm really good at doing nothing. It's one of my better skills."

Riley snorted, then sighed.

"This will all blow over in a few days," I said. "You just wait and see."

Spencer inhaled another wad of French fries. "You don't believe that for a second."

Of course I don't, I almost said, but for once, I kept my mouth shut.

THREE

B Y THE TIME I got home, I was as worn out as an old shoelace. Faking stupidity was tougher than it looked.

Mom could tell something was wrong as soon as I trudged through the door. She was halfway through her Sudoku—they only took her a few minutes—but after taking one look at my face, she set it on the couch. "All right," she said. "Let's hear it."

Mom was lots of things—a former litigator, a Sudoku champion, and a not-so-awesome cook—but most of all, she was Mom. Dad said she could roast any witness in three questions or less, but she said her real talent lay in raising six boys (or at least five and a half, since she wasn't finished raising me).

When I didn't answer, she made a face. "Did Garth empty his spit valve on your shoe again?"

I shook my head. "I think Garth was home sick. He was coughing all over the place yesterday. He probably has pneumonia, which means I'll probably have pneumonia within the next day or two."

Mom half smiled, half sighed. "Is that what's eating you?"

I shook my head again. "I guess I was just…thinking." Under my breath, I added, "I probably don't do that enough."

Mom made a strange noise. It sounded like a laugh, but that couldn't have been what it was. Something must have gotten stuck at the back of her throat.

"Will you at least give me a hint?" she asked when I just stood there thinking.

I pressed my lips into a line, determined not to let it out, but the pressure slowly built until I couldn't keep it in: "I told Riley that Veronica doesn't represent our opinions and that we should, you know, fight, and a few kids overheard me, and now everyone knows."

"Even Veronica?" she asked.

I nodded slowly.

"Oh, David, you know how powerful words can be." She glanced down at her lap. "They can hurt people, you know."

"Not the Pritchard-Pratt," I replied. "She's, like, the queen of ice. I doubt a heat-seeking missile could penetrate her permafrost."

"Most people would seem different if you could see them from the inside."

The truth of her words hit me like a thousand-pound gorilla—I'd always been of the opinion that I was cooler than I looked—but I pretended that they hadn't. "She didn't *seem* upset. In fact, she challenged me to run against her."

Mom picked up her Sudoku. "Well, then, I think you should."

I shook my head. "No way."

"Why not?" she replied.

"Because that's not the way it works! Don't you remember middle school? The populars win the elections and score the winning baskets, and the BGs play the fight songs and grovel at their feet."

Mom considered that, then shrugged. "Why couldn't someone do both?"

For a second, maybe less, I saw two flashes of Veronica. In the first flash, she was sitting behind the piano, and in the second, she was standing on the populars' table, freezing us with one look.

But Veronica didn't count. She was the exception to every rule.

"Because you can't," I said emphatically, then said it once more for good measure: "You just can't do both."

23

"Whatever you say," Mom replied, but I could tell she didn't mean it.

✳   ✳   ✳

I had to shuffle past the office to get to my locker the next morning, which meant I had to shuffle past the dreaded sign-up sheet. It fluttered daringly in the air-conditioned breeze, and I got the impression that it wanted to be seen.

But the sign-up sheet didn't pose even the slightest threat. I wasn't going to give in, so it wasn't an issue. Mom might have been right about most things, but she wasn't right about this.

Instead of waiting for Riley, I headed straight to the band room. It was usually deserted before school, and I could use the practice. When I originally signed up for band, I'd planned to play the tuba, but when we tried out each instrument on the first day of school, I'd struggled to stay upright when it was just sitting on my shoulders. After that, I'd taken the trombone for a test-drive, but my arms hadn't been long enough to fully extend the slide. That was how I'd gotten stuck with my rinky-dink trumpet (which Mr. Ashton had referred to as "the little man's horn"). It wasn't an instrument I was keen to master, but if I ever wanted to graduate to bigger, better things, I had no choice but to play it.

I'd just slipped through the door when I jolted to a stop. The band room wasn't empty. Veronica was sitting on the edge of the woodwinds.

"What are you doing here?" I demanded, tightening my grip on my trumpet case. The handle suddenly felt slippery.

"What does it look like?" she asked.

"It looks like you got lost on your way to the bathroom."

"I don't get lost," she replied, flipping her hair over her shoulder. "I'm always *exactly* where I mean to be."

"All right," I said, taking the bait. "Then why did you *mean* to be here?"

Her shoulders actually slumped. "I don't know," she admitted. "Mr. Ashton asked to see me."

I cupped a hand around my mouth. "Well, in case you haven't noticed, Mr. Ashton isn't here."

Veronica rolled her eyes. "But he should be here any minute. He told me to come early."

If we'd been in a movie, that would have been Mr. Ashton's cue. He would have magically pranced through the door before I was forced to say something. But we weren't in a movie, so he didn't appear. I could have run away, but seeing her sitting there like she owned the place made something in me snap. The band room should have been my territory—I was the BG, not her—and I wasn't going to stand here and let her take over everything.

I hugged my trumpet case and skirted the edge of the band room, then set my stuff next to my chair and lowered myself into my seat. I popped the latches as quietly as I could, but in the suffocating silence, the pops echoed like gunshots. I snuck a peek at Veronica to see if she'd noticed, but she was still just sitting there, making herself as small as possible.

My hands trembled like dead leaves barely clinging to their branches as I tugged my mouthpiece out of its divot. I blew into it once or twice, then slid it into its slot and tapped the valves experimentally. It was more warm-up than I usually did, but she still hadn't moved. Finally, I was down to either playing or talking, so I picked the latter.

"Aren't you curious?" I blurted. I desperately wanted to know if she'd heard what I'd said.

At least that snapped her out of it. "Aren't you?" she replied.

I crinkled my forehead. "About what?"

She folded her arms across her waist. "About why I said what *I* said."

I swallowed, hard. It was like she'd read my mind. How had this conversation spiraled so far out of control? I thought I was the one asking the questions. But then, I *was* curious about the Lunchroom Stand.

"Well, sure," I said nonchalantly. "I think everyone has been wondering why you climbed onto that table."

Veronica waved that away. "The table was a prop. A stepstool would have worked, but I didn't have one handy."

"Trust me," I replied, "you don't need a stepstool."

For a second, maybe less, Veronica's frosty expression slipped, and I winced despite myself. Maybe Mom was right. Maybe Veronica *did* care. But then her features hardened, and I felt a little better. Clearly, my words hadn't affected her. It must have been a trick of the light.

"I'm tired," she said. "Tired of winning by default." She looked me in the eyes. "I'm ready for a blowout."

The look in her eyes burned right through me, and I shrank away from her. If she was looking for a blowout, she'd come to the right place. Except I wasn't going to run. But I didn't have a chance to get those words out before Mr. Ashton strolled into the room, a stack of music in one arm and a box of doughnuts in the other.

"Oh, I'm glad I caught you!" he said. "David, Veronica, why don't you pull up a seat?"

She sent me a sideways glance. "Don't you think you should have mentioned that he asked to see you, too?"

I held up my hands. "He didn't tell me anything!"

"No, I didn't," he replied, but then he ruined it by winking. "Since I knew he'd be here, anyway."

I knotted my arms across my chest. Why did everyone seem to think that they had me figured out? I wasn't that predictable, was I? I tried to kick my music stand, but my kick went to the right, so my foot connected with the back of the piano instead. I had to bite my lip to keep from saying a bad word.

Mr. Ashton set the box of doughnuts on his desk—it sounded mostly empty—then dusted off his hands. "I wanted to talk to you," he went on as he gave her a piece of music, "because I thought you'd like to play something in our upcoming recital."

"But we already are," I said.

"Allow me to rephrase," he replied as he handed me a copy. "I thought you might like to play a duet in our upcoming recital."

Veronica's jaw dropped. "You want us to play *together*?"

Now it was Mr. Ashton's turn to nod. "You and David are my stars!"

I found that hard to believe. "But I don't even like the trumpet."

Mr. Ashton waved that off. "You're a budding Louis Armstrong!"

I crinkled my nose. "Louis *who*?"

"Forget it," he replied as he leafed through his music. When he found the piece he'd given us, he added, "Why don't you just take a look?"

I squinted at the title (which was partially obscured by a smudge of chocolate icing). "'La Vie en rose'?" I read out loud. "That's not even English, right?"

Veronica shook her head. "No, it's French." Under her breath, she added, "Not that *you* would know."

She might have whispered it, but she'd clearly meant for me to hear. I slammed the music down, but before I could come up with a decent reply, Mr. Ashton held his hands up.

"Now, now," he replied. "There's no reason to get testy. I'm not asking you to love it, I'm just asking you to *try*."

I rolled my tongue around my mouth. Veronica didn't react.

Mr. Ashton sighed. "If you come back Monday morning and you absolutely loathe it—really loathe it, not just hate it—maybe we'll try something else. Or just give up altogether." He held the music out like he was offering us his soul. "But at least give it a chance."

Grudgingly, I flipped the music open and played the first few notes in my head. At least it didn't sound too schmaltzy. French music usually was.

Veronica stuffed hers in her bag. "All right," she replied as she made a break for it. Just before she disappeared, she glanced back at me. "But this doesn't change anything. I'm still going to destroy you."

"No, you're not," I said, "because I'm not gonna run!"

"Of course you're not," was all she said, but as she swept away, I thought I could hear her laughter skipping back down the hall.

FOUR

THAT AFTERNOON, THE SCHOOL bus dropped me off at the end of Jacob's Way. The school bus always dropped me off at the end of Jacob's Way, but since it was a Friday, a few notes of Sergei Rachmaninoff, Dad's favorite composer, drifted down the street to greet me.

Dad had been a lawyer, too, back when he and Mom worked on the Frivolous Lawsuit of the Century (or the FL of the C). That was how they'd met all those years and kids ago. Dad had been for the defense, and Mom had been for the plaintiff, but somehow, they'd impressed each other with their legal briefs. Mom's team had won the case, but they'd both made out like buccaneers on their share of the legal fees. As soon as that verdict had been read, they'd given their day jobs the boot and gotten married in Las Vegas (though it hadn't been one of *those* weddings—the ceremony had been private and several miles from the Strip). Mom had taken up Sudoku—she was now on the national team—and Dad had opened a garage.

Classics by Jesse had four bays and a storefront on Main Street, but that hadn't stopped Dad from turning our garage into a workshop complete with a floor jack and a fully stocked tool chest. He closed early on Fridays so his teenage employees could have a social life, so instead of tinkering at work, he spent the rest of the night tinkering in our garage.

"Hey, Dad!" I shouted over Mr. Rachmaninoff's most famous concerto. Dad's shop wasn't called Classics by Jesse just because he had a thing for classic cars. "Do you have a second?"

Dad pushed his goggles back. He looked like a reverse raccoon, with light eyes and dark cheeks. "Sure, Dave. What's on your mind?"

Dad was the only person on the planet who was allowed to call me Dave, but he could only call me that when Mom wasn't around. She thought nicknames were for pets.

"It's just this piece," I replied, wrestling it out of my backpack. I felt kind of guilty as I handed it to him, since his hands were caked with grease, but then, Mr. Ashton had already nailed it with chocolate icing. "Have you ever heard of 'La Vie en rose'?"

Dad whistled under his breath. "Have I heard of it? It's 'La Vie en rose'!"

"Yeah, it's French," I said weakly.

"That's right," he said, nodding. "It literally means 'The life in pink,' but a better English translation would be 'A rosy life' or 'Life through rose-colored glasses.'" When I just stood there blinking, he added, "You know, a perfect life."

"Oh," I replied. That must have been why Veronica liked it so much.

Dad looked over the music. "Edith Piaf wrote it, but Louis Armstrong made it famous."

There was that name again. "Who was he?"

Dad threw up his arms. "Only the most famous man who's ever blown a horn!"

I took the music back before he could fling it far and wide. "So you think it's a good song?"

Dad nodded. "It's the best." He wiped his hands off on a nearby rag (which, now that I thought about it, he probably should have done first), then sent me a sideways glance. "Out of curiosity, where did you get it?"

"From Mr. Ashton," I replied. "He wants me to play it in the recital."

Dad made a show of polishing his socket wrench. "He wants you to play it by yourself?"

I glanced down at my toes. "No, he thinks I should play it with Veronica Pritchard-Pratt."

He set his socket wrench down. "I see."

So he and Mom had been talking. I guess that shouldn't have surprised me. Worry rumbled in my stomach, but I couldn't decide if I was more upset or more relieved.

Dad snuck a peek at me. "So are you going to do it?"

"Play 'La Vie en rose'?" I asked.

He nodded.

"I don't know," I admitted, then sent *him* a sideways glance. "What do you think I should do?"

Dad considered that, then shrugged. "I think you should go for it. I mean, you only get so many chances to play the greats."

"But what about Veronica? How can I work with her after…?"

"You dared each other to a duel?"

I ducked my head. "Yeah, after that."

Instead of answering, he closed the hood of the Dodge Challenger he'd been working on. I'd never understood his obsession with the classics, but even I had to admit that the old girl was a beaut. With her long, sleek body and snub nose, she looked like a great white shark (if great white sharks were pumpkin orange and had black racing stripes). Once he fixed the carburetor and got the transmission up and running, she would be a squeal on wheels.

"I think," Dad finally said, "that the election shouldn't matter. I mean, this will all blow over in another couple of days. It isn't like you're going to run."

It was weird to hear my words coming out of someone else's mouth. Either he'd read my mind, or he'd bugged my lunch box. I didn't want to think about either option for too long.

If Dad noticed my distress, he did a good job of not showing it. "I'll see you in there," he went on as he motioned toward the door. "Tell your mom I'm almost done."

I didn't respond, just nodded vaguely. I was too busy thinking about everything I had to think about, but maybe that was just what he'd been trying to get me to do.

✳ ✳ ✳

I played "La Vie en rose" the first time to hear what it sounded like, but I played it again just because it had intrigued me. It took me a few tries to get the syncopation right, but Dad helped me get it down, sometimes whistling the notes, sometimes pounding them out with his trusty socket wrench. By Sunday night, I couldn't remember a time when I didn't know the song, and even though my low B was shaky, I could say I was in love.

On Monday, I stomped back to the band room to tell Mr. Ashton I would do it. He must have known the song would sway me. But Mr. Ashton wasn't there. Why did that not surprise me?

I sat down in my usual seat and pulled out my trumpet. I didn't need the music anymore, so I left it in my backpack and focused on the beat: long one, and three, and four, long one, and three, and four—

"The counting is a nightmare," a familiar voice cut in, "but I think you've mastered it."

I cut the music off with an elephantlike wheeze. That note hung in the air like a bad taste in your mouth, but Veronica paid it no heed.

"Good morning to you, too," she added as she swished through the door.

I cradled my trumpet. "I didn't think you'd come back and risk your reputation."

"And I didn't think you'd follow through, so I guess that means we're even."

"It's 'La Vie en rose,'" I said, shrugging.

Veronica shrugged, too. *Of course it is,* her shoulders

36

seemed to say. Or maybe her shoulders had meant, *I wasn't talking about "La Vie en rose."*

I shifted uncomfortably. Why Veronica had the power to make me feel inferior when she was the one risking her reputation, I couldn't have said.

Before I had a chance to figure out how I was feeling, she glanced up at the clock. "Well, I've got to go." She flicked her hair over her shoulder. "It's May second, you know."

I racked my brains to figure out why the date was so important. Was it some obscure holiday that the populars had made up? I wouldn't have put it past them.

I must have made a face, because Veronica rolled her eyes. "You know, May second?" she went on. "The last day to sign up for the seventh-grade election?"

"You're *reminding* me?" I asked.

"As I already told you," she replied, "I'm tired of winning by default."

I folded my arms across my chest. "Well, I hate to disappoint, but I'm not playing your game."

"Of course you're not," she said. She was halfway out the door before she turned back and added, "Tell Mr. Ashton I'll do it."

I leaped out of my seat. "You don't have to play with me. I can do another song—or find another pianist!" When I realized I was shouting, I blushed and sat back down. "Or Mr. Ashton can, anyway."

"I'm not doing it for you," she said. "I'm doing it for 'La Vie en rose.'" Under her breath, she added, "And your technique isn't *that* bad."

I couldn't decide whether that was a compliment or an insult, but what was even worse was that I couldn't decide which one I wanted it to be.

* * *

Even though I dodged that sign-up sheet like a bad case of the flu, I couldn't get it out of my head. Why had she reminded me about that stupid deadline? Did she really want me in the race, or was she just trying to throw me off? And if she *did* want me in the race, should I run the other way?

Dad and Spencer seemed to think I didn't have it in me, and Veronica had made it sound like she already knew I wouldn't do it. I'd heard people talk about reverse psychology, and though I'd never been clear on exactly what it was, I got the impression that they were using it on me.

By the end of seventh period, I was officially freaking out. A part of me wanted to flee, but another part wanted to wander past the office and see if someone had signed up. Riley seemed oblivious, so when he asked me if I was ready to go, I could have just gone. But instead of nodding, I said, "Oh, no, you go ahead. I'll have to catch up."

Spencer would have grilled me for details—he was going to make a great dad someday—but Riley wasn't Spencer, so he just shrugged and said, "Fine."

I almost told him right there, then changed my mind at the last second. I probably could have handled Riley's powers of persuasion, but if he went and got Spencer, I was going to be doomed.

I waited for him to turn the corner, then counted to thirty by threes and took off in the opposite direction. I tried to fake indifference by whistling "La Vie en rose," but it turned out to be a waste. No one even glanced my way.

The commons was a ghost town littered with clumps of eraser and the partially digested remains of someone's spaghetti. I had to plug my nose to keep from gagging. Rumor had it that Olivia Fitch, who was less good at running than she was at playing Ping-Pong, had barfed on her way from the gym to the nurse's office. Clearly, those rumors were true.

My scoutmaster once taught us how to silently stalk prey, so I put that skill to good use as I crept across the commons. But it was hard to do anything with as much gear as I had, so I set down my trumpet case, then my backpack. With my stuff spread out behind me like a trail of geeky breadcrumbs, I might as well have hung a neon sign over my head: DAVID GRAINGER IS RIGHT HERE.

I was six steps from my goal when a flock of giggling seventh graders burst onto the scene. At first, I tried to freeze, but then it occurred to me that they probably had better eyesight than a Tyrannosaurus rex. I pretended to pick a scab instead, crossing my eyes in concentration. Luckily, they scurried off before I was forced to eat it.

Once the Giggle Girls vanished, I took off at full gallop. There was no more time for stealth; I had to get in and get out as quickly as possible. When I finally reached the door, I wrenched a pencil from my pocket and pressed it against the sign-up sheet. Veronica's name looked so official that I wished I'd brought a pen, but there was no going back now. If I went back, I knew I wouldn't come this way again.

I wrote a crooked *D*, but I was too shaky to finish. As I tried to stretch out my hand, my mind raced back over the last couple of days. If I finished writing my name, there'd be no going back. I'd forever be the BG who'd tried—and failed—to beat Veronica. Was *that* the legacy I wanted to leave?

Then again, what legacy would I leave if I chickened out now?

I drew a shaky breath, then set my fist against the door. But before I could sign my name, the door opened from the inside, and I stabbed myself in the eye with the blunt end of my pencil.

The woman who'd opened the door covered her mouth with both hands. "Oh, I'm so sorry!" she squeaked. "I didn't poke your eye out, did I?"

I massaged my right eye (which was getting sorer by the second). "No," I replied, "but I think my pencil did."

She glanced over her shoulder. "I'm afraid Edna left early, but maybe I could find some ice…"

"It's all right," I said, blinking. Tears were gushing down my face, but I paid them no heed. "I'll get some when I get home."

The squeaky woman, whose name might have been Ms. Marsden, fiddled with her necklace. "Oh, I feel terrible, just terrible. I wish I could do something for you." She glanced down at my pencil, then back up at the sign-up sheet. "Were you trying to join the race?"

I opened my mouth to answer, but no sound came out.

The woman, Maybe Ms. Marsden (hereafter known as the MMM), gave my soggy cheek a pat. "It's okay," she said (though I hadn't said anything myself). "I have a hard time getting my words to come out, too." She scooped up my pencil and scribbled down my name. "It is David, isn't it? I try to memorize the yearbook, but I'm afraid this old noggin isn't what it used to be."

I rolled my tongue around my mouth to get the spit flowing again. "Yeah, I'm David," I mumbled.

She smiled sympathetically. She must have just noticed the name above mine. "Of course you are," she said, then ripped the sign-up sheet off the door. "Now go home and get some ice!"

She slammed the door shut in my face, leaving me to gape at the scrap of sign-up sheet that was still stuck to the door. I didn't usually meet people who talked as much as I did. They knocked me off my game.

As I backed away from the office, I tested my eye. It would probably be tender for at least a day or two, but as the youngest of six boys, I'd definitely had worse. With any luck, I'd wake up with a killer black eye (and a tall tale to go with it), but for now, I was content. My method might have been unorthodox, but I was in the race.

FIVE

I DIDN'T TELL ANYONE WHAT I'd done—not Mom or Dad, not Riley, and definitely not Veronica. But I hadn't taken morning announcements into account. The MMM delivered them almost every day at the start of second period:

"And we'd like to invite everyone who signed up for the seventh-grade election to meet in Ms. Clementi's room for the last fifteen minutes of seventh period. One more time, that's David Grainger and Veronica Pritchard-Pratt to Ms. Clementi's room for the last fifteen minutes of seventh period."

The intercom's parting click left a vacuum of silence that no one dared to fill. But then someone yelled, "Go, David!" which gave the other kids permission to whoop and holler.

I felt my cheeks get hot, but I couldn't stop smiling, since the BGs were going crazy and Mr. Ashton was looking at me like I'd somehow made him proud.

I might have been going crazy, too, if it hadn't been for *her*.

Lesser mortals might have flinched, but Veronica was a god. While the BGs stomped and catcalled and generally made fools of themselves, she just sat there staring, her long neck curved like a swan's, and I got the impression that I'd played right into her hands.

But it was too late to take it back, and as I sailed through the day, I didn't really want to. For the first time in my life, I had a chance to make a mark, leave a piece of myself behind that later travelers might notice. Just because Veronica had essentially goaded me into it wouldn't make it less meaningful.

But if Veronica *had* wanted me to enter the race, she obviously hadn't told her henchmen. As soon as I entered the lunchroom, Hector sidled up to me on one side, and Samantha closed in on the other.

"Davy, Davy," Hector said, draping an arm around my neck, "I think we need to talk."

My heart thumped like a snare drum, but at least my voice didn't squeak. "I'm sorry," I said as I wriggled out of his grip, "but you must have the wrong guy. My name's David, not Davy."

"Potato, po-tah-toe," he replied at the same time Samantha demanded, "Is there a problem here?"

I glanced up at Samantha, who had to outweigh me by at least fifty pounds, and carefully shook my head. She was a bruiser, though she'd been a string bean back in kindergarten. She'd also been one of five or six Samanthas, which was why the teachers had renamed her Samantha P. The chants that had followed her around the playground had practically written themselves: *Look, it's Samantha Pee! Do you like to pee, Samantha Pee? How do you poop, Samantha Pee?*

Too bad no one had realized that Samantha was the niece of the legendary Edgar Pearce, middleweight boxing champion of the Intermountain West, and that she'd soon outgrow the rest of us by a factor of three. No one had used that nickname since the end of the third grade.

But now that I thought about it, I didn't think Veronica ever had. Not that *that* meant anything. Veronica must have ignored her because she ignored everyone.

Before Samantha had a chance to introduce me to her fists, Hector steered me toward the office. "Come on, Davy," he said, slinging his arm around my neck again. "Why don't we cross your name off that pesky sign-up sheet?"

I managed to escape his headlock, but I could still

feel my pulse pounding in my right eye (which, unfortunately, hadn't bruised). "Sorry, Hector," I replied, "but the MMM said it's too late."

I had no idea whether it was too late or not, but sometimes the truth needed a little embellishment. Unfortunately, my embellishment still wasn't enough. When I made a break for my table, Samantha seized my arm and twisted it behind my back.

If you wanted to be a popular, there were only two ways to get in. The first was to be really good at something that most people thought was cool, like basketball or breakdancing. That was how Brady and Veronica had become populars. The second was a little messier. It involved standing beside the velvet rope that separated the populars from the masses and making sure the deadbeats never crossed it.

I guess it was pretty obvious how Hector and Samantha had gotten in.

Samantha's breath was hot on my neck. "We can do this the easy way, or we can do this the hard way."

"What's the hard way?" I asked before I thought better of it, but deep down, I was thinking, *Oh, please, oh, please, oh, please.*

Samantha bared her teeth. Her nails dug crescent moons into my arm, but when I tried to yank it away, they only sank in deeper. "The hard way," she said slowly, like she was savoring the description, "involves finding a toilet and—"

"Let him go, Samantha."

I didn't recognize the voice that had momentarily delayed my fate, and judging by the puzzled looks on Hector's and Samantha's faces, they didn't recognize it, either. Cautiously, we turned around. Esther Lambert, who I'd talked to maybe twice in my whole life, had come to my rescue. Her knees were bent, her shoulders were square, and she was brandishing a pencil like a rapier.

Esther was in newspaper with Riley and me, but since she was a designer and I was a reporter (which wasn't as cool as it sounded), we'd never had to exchange words or even get within three feet of one another's personal space. I never would have guessed that she'd take on the populars. She'd never struck me as a fighter.

Samantha squeezed my arm, cutting off my circulation. "Bug off," was all she said.

Esther grabbed my other arm. At least she cut her nails every so often. "No, you bug off," she said.

Samantha's ears flamed scarlet, but she didn't bug off. "What did you say?" she asked as her other hand clenched into a fist.

I would have taken one look at that fist and headed back the way I'd come, but Esther stood her ground. "Are you sure you want to do that?"

Samantha's sneer faltered. I couldn't help but be impressed. No one had stood up to Samantha since she'd hit her first growth spurt.

"Hector, do something!" she hissed.

But Hector just held up his hands. "Girls are your problem, *muchacha*."

"You're such a wimp," she said, but before she could cock her fist, a shadow fell over our shoes.

It was too tall to be anyone's but Veronica's.

"Let them go," she commanded.

I forced myself not to yelp as Samantha let go of my arm. If she'd held on for another minute, they probably would have had to amputate. Still, I was going to have crescent moon–shaped indents embedded in my skin for hours.

Veronica sniffed. "I want a cookie."

Hector and Samantha exchanged a confused glance. Either this request was a strange one, or they were dumber than they looked.

"I said, I want a cookie." She pulled a dollar bill from her pocket and waved it under their noses. "Oatmeal raisin, preferably. Otherwise, a chocolate chip."

Hector opened his mouth to argue, but Samantha dragged him away before he could get the words out. Esther hopped out of their way and offered them a courtly bow (which they purposely ignored). I tried not to wince as I massaged my injured arm, but I didn't fool Veronica.

"Did she hurt you?" she whispered.

Instinctively, I dropped my arm. "Oh, no, I'm all right."

"Are you kidding?" Esther asked. "She practically ripped your arm off!"

"I said, I'm all right," I growled. I didn't want Veronica to think that I was a first-rate wimp.

Veronica half nodded, half shrugged. "I'm still sorry," she said. "They shouldn't have manhandled you."

I felt my cheeks get hot. Did that mean she thought I was a man? But she didn't give me a chance to ask, just headed over to her table. I headed over to my table, too, where Riley and Spencer were pretending to be captivated by the fake wood grain. I was nearly there when I remembered to thank Esther. I glanced over my shoulder—she was probably finding a seat over at the artists' table—but she was right behind me.

"Oh, there you are," I mumbled as I tipped over backward. Luckily, the bench broke my fall. Without meeting her gaze, I added, "Thank you for your help back there."

"You're welcome," she replied, then plopped down on the bench beside me.

I wasn't sure how to react. No girl had ever sat at our table before. Maybe if we pretended not to notice, she'd get tired and leave.

Unfortunately, Spencer was less patient. "Beat it, Esther," he said, pointing a Cheeto at her head. He'd always had a way with women.

Esther stuck her chin out. "No."

Spencer frowned. "Please beat it?"

"*No*," she said again. "I'm here because I want to help."

Spencer huffed. "Help with *what*?"

"With the campaign, of course. And with the security detail, since you two clearly aren't capable of keeping our candidate alive."

At least Spencer had the decency to duck his head. "Why do you want to help?" he asked.

"Why do you think?" Esther replied. "David's the best chance we've got of taking down Veronica's dynasty."

Riley glared at his carrot sticks. "He's the *only* chance," he said, "because no one else was dumb enough to take the populars on."

"*She* took them on just now," I said.

"But I didn't sign up for the race." Esther nudged me with her elbow. "That was a stroke of genius, by the way."

I blushed down to my toes, but either Spencer didn't notice, or he just didn't care.

"That's the only reason?" he replied. "You're not fishing for a student council seat?"

Esther crinkled her nose. "Why would I want one of those?"

Instead of sneering, Spencer blinked. "Then I guess we'll think about it."

I started to point out that *I'd* be making the decisions, but before I could get the words out, Riley shouted, "WHAT?"

We all looked at him like he'd grown a thirteenth toe (since he already had twelve).

He looked at Spencer like he'd shot him. "I thought you didn't support this!"

Instead of blushing, Spencer shrugged. "It's like my uncle always says—if you can't beat them, lead them."

Not that Spencer's uncle was a beacon of what-to-do-ness—he was currently serving ten to twenty for mortgage and investment fraud—but in this case, he had a point.

Esther made a face. "Who died and made you campaign manager?"

"What campaign?" Riley moaned, plopping his chin into his hands. "Veronica is going to trounce him."

I knotted my arms across my chest. "Thanks for that vote of confidence." Then I set my sights on Spencer. "And I thought you *were* against this."

"That was, like, last week," he said. "Can't a guy change his mind?"

Riley stuck his chin out. "*No.*"

"I'm still waiting to find out why you get to be the leader," Esther said.

"Because I have a vision." Spencer leaned forward and lowered his voice. "Veronica doesn't win because she's good, she wins because she's popular, so we just have to figure out how to make David populager."

Riley made a face. "'Populager' isn't a word."

Spencer tried to argue, but I beat him to the pause.

"It doesn't matter," I replied, "because it isn't possible. Veronica is and always will be the queen of the populars."

Spencer rubbed his jaw. "But they've never played the game *our* way."

SIX

SPENCER SPENT THE REST of lunch describing—in very general terms—how we were going to beat Veronica, but every time Esther asked him for specifics, he pretended not to hear. I agreed to make him my campaign manager just to shut him up, but that only fanned the flames. By the time that lunch was over, he'd made Riley my speechwriter and told Esther to beat it (twice). She'd stormed off in a huff.

Spencer's bullheadedness had done one thing—it had convinced me this was real. I was actually running for class president. There was no denying it. By the end of seventh period, I honestly couldn't decide if I was more excited or more nervous.

Ms. Clementi's room was more of a museum than a classroom—her pencil stub collection took up one wall by itself—but at least it was familiar. Riley had signed up for band for me, so I'd signed up for newspaper for him. Ms. Clementi might have been a screwball, but at least she let us do our own things.

She looked up from her phone when I slid into my seat. "Good afternoon," she said like we were sitting down to tea. "I was very pleased to hear that you'd signed up for the election."

I swallowed, hard. "You were?"

"Yes," Ms. Clementi said. "Why, it's not every day that a member of my staff campaigns for office."

"Oh, well," I said, blushing, "I kind of signed up on a whim. Well, *actually,* the MMM signed up on a whim for me. But she did use my pencil."

She returned her attention to her phone. It was embarrassing to think that Ms. Clementi, who'd probably known Alexander Graham Bell personally, had a phone when I didn't. "How nice," she said pleasantly. "It will be a shame when that Pritchard-Pratt girl kills you."

I felt the blood drain from my cheeks, but before I could defend myself, Veronica walked in. She looked back and forth between us, then sat down in Riley's desk (which was directly behind mine). She must have overheard our conversation, but she managed not to show it.

Ms. Clementi got out of her seat and retrieved two

cumbersome white packets that someone had stapled in the wrong corner. "The rules and regulations," she said brightly as she handed them to us, then perched her glasses on her nose and proceeded to read the first page out loud: "Campaigning may begin as early as tomorrow and may continue until the assembly on the morning of Friday, May twentieth. Voting will take place immediately thereafter, and the winner will be announced by the end of seventh period."

Veronica kicked the back of my seat. "May twentieth," she whispered. "The day after the recital."

I couldn't believe it. It was like my entire life had been leading up to those two days.

"As for campaigning," Ms. Clementi said, "all candidates are allowed to spend fifty dollars on materials such as signs, T-shirts, and handouts." She squinted at us over her glasses. "Keep in mind that these materials should not be inappropriate. And any handouts you distribute may not constitute a bribe. That means no candy, no gum, no merchandise of any kind. Perhaps you've heard of Michael Belcher, who tried to hand out barf bags in the lunchroom. It was disgraceful, just disgraceful." She looked back down at her notes—and giggled. "Funny, but disgraceful."

I grinned despite myself. Michael and Radcliff had

been friends. In fact, I was pretty sure the barf bags had been his idea.

Ms. Clementi's smile vanished. "No barf bags, you understand?"

My smile vanished, too. "Of course not, Ms. Clementi."

"All right, then. Now, where were we?" She scanned the first page of her packet, then flipped it over to the second. "Ah, yes, campaign materials. If any candidate cannot afford the spending limit, then arrangements may be made wherein the school will fund the difference." She eyed Veronica and me again. "Will that apply to either of you?"

I shook my head swiftly. I didn't want to have to mention the FL of the C (which, as Mom was fond of saying, would pay for the lives of many Graingers and possibly the national debt). Veronica must have said no, too, since Ms. Clementi didn't linger. I thought about sneaking a peek at her, then changed my mind at the last second.

"Well, then, I think that covers it." Ms. Clementi set her packet down and rubbed her eyes with baby fists, partially dislodging her glasses. "Now, do you have any questions?"

I flipped through the first few pages, less out of interest than anxiety. It looked like someone had typed it in seven-and-a-half-point font. "Are we supposed to read all this *tonight*? What if we break one of the rules?"

"Oh, well," Ms. Clementi said, "we'd probably pry off all your toenails and make you eat them in a stew."

Veronica half snorted, half choked.

Ms. Clementi laughed maniacally. "Hyperbole!" she said.

I laughed less maniacally. "Hyperbole" was her favorite word, though it had taken me a while to track the definition down (since it wasn't spelled like how it sounded). *Black's Law Dictionary* hadn't had it, but Merriam-Webster had defined it as "language that describes something as better or worse than it really is." Until then, I'd thought it meant "crazy things that English teachers say to shock and horrify their students."

Veronica's desk creaked. "Does that mean you'd kick us out?"

Ms. Clementi made a face. "Good heavens, no. Who do you think we are, the Federal Elections Commission?"

While Ms. Clementi giggled, I leaned back and hissed over my shoulder, "Don't you already know this stuff?"

She didn't lean forward to meet me. "Haven't had to run before, remember?"

"Oh, right," I mumbled sheepishly as I felt my cheeks get hot. I was glad she couldn't see them.

Veronica ignored me. "Ms. Clementi," she said loudly, "if I'm understanding you correctly, we just can't spend too much money, we can't hand out gum or candy, and we shouldn't be morons?"

"Yes," Ms. Clementi said, "I'd say that sums it up."

"Fantastic," she replied as she slid out of her desk. She was halfway out the door before she turned around and asked, "Is it all right if we go?"

I snuck a peek up at the clock. The bell wasn't going to ring for another four minutes and twelve seconds.

"Of course!" Ms. Clementi said, wiggling her fingers at the door. "Just don't let Ms. Quintero catch you. That woman has no sense of humor."

"Oh, don't worry," she replied. "I'm best friends with Ms. Quintero."

Veronica was out the door before I'd even finished sliding the packet into my backpack. I might have acted like tough stuff, but I didn't have any experience with avoiding Ms. Quintero. I managed to kill a few more minutes by zipping up my backpack really slowly, but there were still two minutes left by the time that I was done. With a pounding heart, I crept out into the hall—and almost leaped out of my skin when I ran into Veronica.

"Geez!" I said, falling back. "Are you trying to give a guy a heart attack?"

She didn't apologize for scaring me—but she did apologize. "I just wanted to say that I'm sorry about what happened in the lunchroom." It took me a second to realize that she was talking about Hector and Samantha. "I didn't ask them to do that."

"I'm sure you didn't," I replied, beating a hasty retreat. "They're just naturally awful."

She fell into step beside me. I tried to outpace her, but my ruler-long legs were no match for her yardsticks.

"Overzealous," she replied. "They're overzealous, not awful." Under her breath, she added, "And they have their reasons."

I sent her a sideways glance. "What is that supposed to mean?"

Instead of answering, she shook her head. "They're not my secrets to tell."

I tilted my head to the side. "So what *is* your secret?"

Veronica started to say something, then changed her mind at the last second. "Who said I had one?" she replied, then spun around and stalked away before I had a chance to answer (which was probably just as well).

I just stood there blinking as she disappeared around the corner. I guess the whole encounter really shouldn't have surprised me. If girls were hard to read and populars were complex and mysterious, then I'd never understand the most popular girl who'd ever lived.

Spencer wanted to get started on my campaign materials right away, but I told him they would have to wait. Mom and I had been planning a trip to Trash to Treasure for a week, and I wasn't about to cancel it for something as lame as a poster.

As soon as the ancient door clunked open, a rush of warm air greeted me. The store didn't have an air conditioner (or at least it didn't have a very good one). The swamp cooler in the back pumped slightly cooler humid air through roughly three-fourths of the building, but it had never bothered me. I drew a deep breath through my nose, then blew it back out through my mouth. It smelled like opportunity and Granny Grainger's attic, where Abner, my second oldest brother, had once unearthed the unabridged works of George and Ira Gershwin.

Mom glanced at her watch. "You only have twenty-five minutes. If you need anything before then, I'll be over by the cookbooks."

I forced myself not to grimace. Mom had recently decided that she was a gourmet chef in hiding and that a library of cookbooks would reveal her hidden talents, but if I'd learned anything over the last twelve years, it was that good lawyers didn't necessarily make good cooks.

She punched me in the shoulder. "Happy hunting," she added.

"You, too," I mumbled weakly, though I was lying through my teeth. Secretly, I hoped she didn't come across a sequel to *The Gourmet Goulash*.

While she headed off to Books, I made a beeline for Collectibles. Even though I collected lunch boxes, I'd never thought of them as collectibles, but where else were they going to shelve them, in Housewares or Small Appliances? The only things worth buying in either of those departments were the refurbished blenders, and that was only if you planned to convert them into blender rockets.

They didn't have any more lunch boxes (and they

hadn't for months), so I strolled over to Clothing on the far end of the store. As the youngest of six boys, I'd inherited more hand-me-downs than I could keep in one closet, but I still had nineteen minutes and a hankering to find a T-shirt that had My Little Ponies on it. The quest had once been Radcliff's, but he'd passed it down to me after he'd gotten a real job. Designing skate parks for a living didn't leave him with a lot of time, and I liked feeling connected to my brothers, most of whom had moved out before I was potty-trained.

I wandered into the girls' section, which seemed like the most likely place to find the T-shirt I was looking for, but it wasn't long before I realized there wasn't a single graphic T-shirt in the entire store. The good people of SV clearly had no taste. When I hit the safari prints, I knew it was time to split, but before I could escape, a shadow fell across the aisle.

Rocking a T-shirt with a rainbow-haired pony was one thing, but getting caught shopping for one was another. After drawing a deep breath, I threw myself into a rack of cowboy shirts and settled in for a long wait. I'd gotten used to waiting for things, including puberty, the bathroom, and Taco Tuesday (which was the one night a week that Mom didn't insist on cooking). I was sure I could outlast whoever that shadow belonged to.

"Do you see something you like, Ronny?"

I had to bite my lip to keep from squealing. There was only one girl in SV who could have a nickname like Ronny, and she was the very last person I wanted to run into right now.

"Not really," Veronica said. "I mean, this tunic's okay." A nearby rack rustled. "But it's still kind of…"

"Gross?" the gravelly voice finished. I couldn't see the man that the gravelly voice belonged to, but he was probably looking at these cowboy shirts.

"I wasn't going to say that," she murmured.

The man's shoe squeaked as if he'd shifted awkwardly. I shifted awkwardly, too, but not because of what she'd said. These cowboy shirts were itchy, and at least one of them smelled like the inside of a barn.

"I'm sorry," the man said. "Sorry I can't take you to—"

"You don't have to apologize. It is what it is. There's no sense jawing about it."

There was an uncomfortable pause before the man finally said, "Your mother says that."

"Yeah, well, she says lots of things."

This conversation might have gone on indefinitely if it hadn't been for the Almighty Sneeze. I tried to hold it in, but this sneeze was so almighty that it came out, anyway. It rattled the whole rack of cowboy shirts (which promptly spit me back out).

The man swore under his breath, but it was Veronica's response that made me want to shrivel up and die: "David, is that you?"

I pushed myself back to my feet, caking my hands with dust and grit. "I guess there's no denying it."

She drew herself up to her full height. "Were you spying on me?" she asked.

"Of course not," I replied, brushing the grit off my hands. I pretended to inspect one of the cowboy shirts "Yeah, I'd say this blend is sixty-three-percent fake."

Veronica wasn't impressed. "What are you doing here?" she demanded.

I thought about telling the truth, then immediately thought better of it. "It's probably better if you don't know."

My eyes flicked to the man who was standing beside her. I started at his shoes (steel-toed work boots that were slightly smaller than huge), then worked my way up to his hair (thinning, light brown, and greasy). He had to be seven feet tall—which made him Veronica's dad.

"Were you in the NBA?" I blurted.

"What's the NBA?" he asked.

I scuffed my foot. "You know, the National Basketball Association?" Or at least that was what I thought it stood for. Elias, my oldest brother, would have been able to say for sure. "Did you used to play?"

The man sniffed. "I don't play anything—not tiddly-winks, not board games, and definitely not basketball." He sent Veronica a sideways glance. "Games are for fancy folks who want to get into important schools, and fancy folks and Pratts have never mixed and never will."

"Oh," I mumbled lamely. But maybe he wasn't her dad. "So you aren't Mr. Pritchard-Pratt?"

The man gritted his teeth. "No, my name's Mr. Pratt. Ms. Pritchard is my...wife."

"Oh," I mumbled again. I'd thought that moms and dads had to have the same last name.

Veronica grabbed her dad's arm. "We should go," she said bluntly, tightening her grip on a purple shirt that Mom probably would have called a blouse.

"Are you gonna buy that?" I replied.

She glanced down at the shirt like she couldn't remember how she'd ended up with it, then returned it to its hanger. "Of course not," she replied. "I've seen better tunics at the mall."

Mr. Pratt's eyes hardened. "Ronny, you know we can't—"

"I *know*." She gave her dad the stink eye. "I just don't want this one. Can't a girl change her mind?"

We both knew better than to answer that question.

"Come on," she told Mr. Pratt. "Mom's probably home by now."

She didn't look back as she strutted away, long, blond hair swinging behind her. Mr. Pratt gave me one last look, then raced to catch up with his daughter. His steel toes tapped indignantly across the linoleum.

Mom passed them on the walkway. "Finished?" she asked blithely.

I swallowed, hard. "Sure."

She motioned toward the purple shirt. "Were you going to get that one?" she asked.

I made a face. "Give me a break."

"Hey, it's your loss," she said (though she was trying not to smile). "I think you would look good in purple."

"Gross, Mom. That's just gross." I shivered despite myself. "Purple *isn't* my color."

But as I followed her to the registers, I couldn't help but wonder if it might be Veronica's.

SEVEN

A S SOON AS WE pulled up to our house, a plain-
looking brown rambler on the northeast side of
town, I spotted Riley and Spencer, who were waiting on the porch. When I said we'd get together later,
they must have taken it literally. I was still trudging up
the walk when Spencer launched into a rant about the
evils of plaid flannel. It would have been an awesome
opportunity to mention my run-in with Veronica, but
he didn't stop to take a breath until I'd produced my
keys, unlocked the door, and silently ushered them in.
Besides, it felt weird to talk about Veronica when she
couldn't defend herself, so I just kept my mouth shut.

At least Spencer shut up when I announced that
I was ready to make my campaign materials. Mom
provided the supplies (a few posters, some dried-up
markers, and an old paint-by-numbers kit), Spencer
organized us into stations, and Riley came up with the
slogans—which left the painting to me.

By the time that we were done, we'd spilled the paint-by-numbers kit all over the back patio, but we'd also produced a couple of somewhat decent posters. But when we got to school on Tuesday, we knew that even Riley's best slogan, "This Grainger Ain't No Stranger," wasn't going to cut it.

If I'd had to guess, I would have said that Veronica's poster—if you could even call it that—was twenty feet tall, with golden trim and one red tassel dangling from its pointed end (which was practically scraping the floor). I wasn't sure how she'd attached it, but it was hanging from the rafters like a banner in a throne room. It only said one thing—VERONICA PRITCHARD-PRATT, 7TH-GRADE CLASS PRESIDENT, with a larger-than-life picture of Veronica herself—but it said it so emphatically that I couldn't help but swallow. It wasn't a slogan; it was a simple statement of fact.

I chucked my poster on the floor, then gave it a swift kick for good measure.

Spencer didn't seem to notice. "What *is* that thing?" he asked.

"It's defeat," Riley replied, collapsing onto his trombone case.

Spencer managed to ignore him. "Doesn't that break one of the rules?"

"I don't think so," I admitted. She wouldn't have been dumb enough to spend more than fifty bucks.

Riley plopped his chin into his hands. "So what are we going to do?"

I glanced down at the poster that I'd kicked across the commons. Compared to Veronica's banner, it looked like a kindergartner's art project. "I don't know," I mumbled.

"Well, I do," a voice said.

We turned around in unison, our faces frozen in shock. Esther was standing behind us, and her hands were on her hips.

"You're gonna dump all of those eyesores in that garbage over there"—she flicked a thumb over her shoulder—"and then you're gonna make me art director of this bumbling campaign."

I cocked an eyebrow. "Just like that?"

"Just like that," Esther replied, tucking her arms across her waist. "Or do you want to be the only kid at Shepherd's Vale who's never won a single vote?"

"Oh, that's cold," Spencer said, but instead of dismissing her, he sighed. "Look, we appreciate the offer, but my candidate and I are gonna have to think about it."

"Actually," I said, "I don't think we need to think

about anything." I held out my hand to Esther. "Welcome to the team."

Esther beamed as we shook hands, but Spencer sputtered like a leaky faucet.

"But I'm the campaign manager!" he said. "You can't hire someone without my say-so!"

"I'm pretty sure I can," I said. "And I'm pretty sure I just did."

Esther scooped up our old posters and dumped them brusquely in the trash. "Fantastic," she replied as she dusted off her hands. "Now we can get to work."

✲ ✲ ✲

Esther's first task as art director was to get Ms. Clementi to agree to let us work on my campaign materials instead of next month's newspaper. I'd always thought that Esther was Ms. Clementi's favorite student (or at least I'd thought that since she'd said, *Esther, you're my favorite student*). We didn't make a ton of progress, though Esther spent the whole class scribbling. When the bell finally rang, she confirmed that we hadn't blown her budget on "our experiment in finger paints," then slipped away with a vague promise that she'd have something in the morning.

I managed not to think about the election or anything related to it for the rest of the day, but on my way out to the bus, I accidentally crossed paths with Veronica. She was waiting for me in the commons, directly underneath her banner.

"David," she said sharply as soon as I came into view. I was surprised that she would talk to me—and call me by name—in front of so many other people. "We need to practice our duet."

"Yeah, sure," I said distractedly. Practicing for the spring recital was the last thing on my mind.

"You don't understand," she said as she hooked me by my backpack straps. "We need to practice it *tonight*."

"Okay, tonight," I said. Was she hard to read? You bet. Complex and mysterious? No doubt about it. "But I'll have to ask my mom."

Veronica nodded. "Fine." She pressed a Post-it Note into my hand. "Just call me once you know. As soon as you know, you understand?" She turned to go, then turned right back. "But we're going to have to practice at your place. I can't have people over at my house."

"Yeah, sure," I said again, though I wasn't really listening anymore. I'd stopped listening as soon as she'd pressed that Post-it Note into my hand. No girl had ever given me her number.

Veronica nabbed the Post-it Note. "You do have a piano, don't you?"

"Of course we do," I said. It had been eleven years since Abner had moved out, but my second oldest brother was still a celebrity around these parts. Every time he came to visit, old ladies bombarded us with cakes and casseroles just so they could hear him play. "But do we have to do this *now*?"

"Yes," was all she said as she smacked me on the chest. I didn't see the Post-it Note stuck to my T-shirt until she was already gone.

* * *

Mom didn't have a problem with the practice; she even dialed the number for me. I'd wanted to text Veronica so I wouldn't have to talk, but Mom hadn't let me borrow her phone. I was the only twelve-year-old on this side of the equator who didn't have his own, but my parents didn't care. *Sacrifice builds character* had to be their favorite slogan.

And that was how, forty-five minutes and one awkward phone call later, I found myself anxiously waiting for Veronica to show. I'd camped out in my room so I wouldn't be hovering by the door (and so I could watch for her, though I'd never admit as much out loud).

I flipped my blender rocket on and off while I kept an eye on the window. The blender rocket had been Owen's—he'd built it for a science fair, and it could fly as high as thirty feet—but then, most of my stuff had belonged to one brother or another. My T-shirts had been Radcliff's (though my boxers were my own). Elias's Michael Jordan posters covered one wall of my room, and Nathan's superhero sketches covered two of the other three. Abner had taken most of his stuff when he moved out of the house, but the CDs he hadn't wanted—and a few of the ones he had—were sitting on the bookcase next to his old stereo. Sometimes I wasn't sure if I was me or bits of them, but since they were the coolest guys I knew, it didn't bug me either way.

I was so busy deciding how much juice to give the blender rocket if I wanted it to graze the ceiling that I didn't notice her pull up (though I did catch a glimpse of her green messenger). I didn't jump up to get the door even after the bell rang, so when Mom didn't get it, either, I had to gallop down the stairs and hope she hadn't walked away.

"Hey," I said, panting. With any luck, she'd think that I'd just been working out.

Veronica dipped her head. "Hello."

I squinted down the street. "How did you get here?" I replied. Jacob's Way looked awfully quiet.

"I took the bus," she said. "You should give it a try sometime."

I made a face. "No, thanks. The school bus is bad enough. I've heard people actually pee on—"

"David!" Mom cut in as she clapped me on the shoulder.

I yelped despite myself. My shoulder was still sore from all of the congratulating.

"I'm sorry," Mom replied, bumping me out of the way. She smiled at Veronica. "Would you like to come in?"

"Yes, thank you," she replied as she stepped across the threshold.

Mom held out her hand. "You must be Veronica."

She shook Mom's hand feebly. "And you must be Ms. Grainger."

"Mrs. Grainger," Mom replied. "I haven't been Ms. Anything since I left the law firm years ago."

Veronica's eyes bulged. "You're a lawyer?"

Mom shrugged. "Well, I was."

Veronica shook her head. She must have been wondering how a lawyer had given birth to a musician as miraculous as I was. I wanted to inform her that Mom was pretty cool (for a mom), but that would have compromised the little bits of reputation I'd managed to scrape together.

I fiddled with my sleeve. "As much as I'd like to sit around and chat about my mom's old lawyer days, we should probably get going." The sooner we ran through "La Vie en rose," the sooner Veronica could leave.

Mom bowed with a flourish. "Shall I unbury the piano?"

Veronica looked back and forth between us. "What do you mean, 'unbury it'?"

"Oh, you know," Mom said as she breezed into the piano room (which she and Dad had made by knocking out an inconvenient wall), "they do take up a lot of space. And when you don't have someone playing them…"

She trailed off when we reached it. It looked less like a piano and more like a sleeping monster with an old drape for a sheet. Stacks of cookbooks, piles of junk mail, and one of Dad's old Phillips screwdrivers rested on every flat surface, and the dust was thick enough that it resembled dingy snow.

Mom sighed dramatically as she retrieved a stack of

cookbooks. "I keep trying to get David to take up the piano, too, but he won't listen to reason."

I crinkled my nose. "Abner's our piano man."

"Well, who said a family couldn't have more than one?" Mom asked as she tugged off the dusty drape and unearthed the shiny Steinway. She surveyed it with pursed lips. "I hope it isn't out of tune."

Veronica tested middle C. It only sounded slightly earsplitting. "It's lovely," she replied.

"No, it's horrible," I said as I unlatched my trumpet case. "Let's just get this over with."

Mom tugged my ear. "Be nice. This young lady is your guest."

"No," I said, "she's my opponent."

Mom rolled her eyes good-naturedly, but when she cupped my chin, her grip was bone-achingly tight. "*Be nice*," she said again, "or I might just have to ground you."

I jerked away from her. I hated it when she cupped my chin; it made me feel like a three-year-old.

"And stop acting like a three-year-old," Mom called over her shoulder as she disappeared into the kitchen, "or I might start treating you like one!"

I felt my cheeks get hot, but Veronica didn't seem to notice (or if she did, she didn't mention it).

"Your mom seems nice," she said.

"She's a mom," I said, scowling. "Don't they kind of have to be?"

Instead of answering, Veronica spread out her music and sat down at the piano. I perched on a nearby chair and freed my trumpet from its case. While I warmed up my mouthpiece, she traced the letters that spelled STEINWAY, then trailed her hands along the keys. The way she touched the keys made me think that they were sacred (or at least that she thought they were). The air suddenly felt charged, but whether with dread or anticipation, I honestly couldn't have said.

As the charge built up inside me, I knew I had to let it out or risk spontaneously combusting, so of course, I said the first thing that popped into my head: "That's a nice banner you've got."

She glared at me across the Steinway. "It didn't cost more than fifty bucks, if *that's* what you're trying to say."

I held up my hands. "I was only making conversation."

That wasn't strictly true, of course, but if I'd come right out and said, *No, what I'm trying to say is that your campaign is gonna murder mine,* she probably wouldn't have believed me.

Veronica's shoulders slumped. "Mom thought I

should get the big one—make a statement, you know? And she knew the guy at the print shop…"

Instead of finishing that thought, Veronica glanced down at her lap. I could have sworn her cheeks reddened, but I only caught a glimpse of them before her hair fell across her face.

"They went out for a while," she explained, "so he said he owed my mom a favor. He only charged us forty-five. I can show you the receipt."

I shook my head. "No, I trust you." That wasn't strictly true, either, but I would have said anything— and I mean, *anything*—to keep from hearing more about her mom and Print Shop Guy.

She straightened her music (though it hadn't needed to be straightened). "Well, what about your signs?"

"What about them?" I asked, stalling.

"Where'd you put them?" she replied.

I scratched the back of my head. I probably could have lied, but the truth was even better. "I didn't, actually. They're at the bottom of the trash can in the middle of the commons."

She half chuckled, half choked. "Is that supposed to be a joke?"

Instead of answering, I shrugged. It was a shrug I'd learned from Nathan, who'd once worked on a sidewalk-chalked landscape on the back patio for months. *Don't bother me with silly questions,* my shoulders seemed to say. *Haven't you ever heard of a work-in-progress?*

But she didn't take the hint. "Where are they really?" she replied.

"I don't know," I admitted. "They're kind of Esther's responsibility."

Or at least I hoped they were. For a second, maybe less, I considered the horrifying possibility that Esther had taken our money and run, then pushed that thought out of my head. We hadn't given Esther any cash, and even if we had, where was she going to run? She wouldn't make it very far on the old bike she rode to school.

Veronica nodded knowingly. "Well, that sounds promising," she said (which was probably a lie, but she said it so convincingly it was hard to say for sure). "Are you ready to begin?"

I slid my mouthpiece into its slot. "As ready as I'll ever be."

"Should we take it from the top, or is there a part you're iffy on?"

I was iffy about the second note and everything that came after it, but I'd told them I would do it, so

I had to follow through. "Let's take it from the top," I said, "and see how far we get."

Veronica eased into the intro, and I came in on the second line. Her piano skipped across the notes like a smooth rock across a pond, my trumpet bouncing in her wake. Our easy blend surprised me. Two middle school band students weren't supposed to sound this good.

We made it through the repeat without stopping even once. As the final notes faded away, we just sat there, barely breathing. That had sounded *good.* I couldn't decide if it was Edith Piaf or Veronica or both, but the only thing I knew for sure was that it definitely wasn't me. I'd been playing "La Vie en rose" for days, and it had never sounded like that, with all its cracks and holes filled in.

Veronica glanced up at me. It was weird to be above her. "Is there a part you want to work on?"

"No," I said carefully. I didn't want to break the spell. "I want to play it just like that again."

We played "La Vie en rose" five more times before Veronica announced that she had to catch the bus. She'd scooted the bench out of the way and was leaping to her feet before I could lower my trumpet.

"Whoa," I said. "Where's the fire? I'm sure the bus driver won't leave you."

"This isn't a school bus," she replied as she gathered up her music and stuffed it back into her bag.

I opened my mouth to answer, but I couldn't get a word out before she hitched her bag over her shoulder and made a beeline for the door. When she slammed it shut behind her, the windows rattled nervously. It was the only evidence that she'd been here at all.

"What the heck was *that*?" I asked as I threw up my arms. I'd heard of kissing and running, but we'd only played a song.

Mom poked her head into the room. "Is everything all right?" she asked.

I returned my trumpet to its case. "Oh, yeah, everything's fine." I wasn't going to admit that I'd been having a good time. "I just didn't think the Pritchard-Pratt would scurry out of here."

Mom glanced out the window, but Veronica had already disappeared. "Give her a break," she said. "Something tells me that that girl has more than a few balls to juggle." She motioned toward our cordless phone. "Oh, and someone called while you were practicing. It sounded like a girl."

"*Another* one?" I asked.

Mom nodded seriously (though one corner of her mouth did twitch). "She said that her name was Esther and that she wants you guys to meet her outside the school first thing tomorrow." She stuck both hands on her hips, but the fact that she was smiling kind of ruined the effect. "Do I need to be concerned?"

"Oh, probably," I said, then scurried out of there myself. What I didn't say was that, for once, I was actually telling the truth.

EIGHT

T HE NEXT MORNING FOUND Riley, Spencer, and me loitering outside the middle school. Spencer kept checking the time, but Esther kept not showing up. Apparently, our definition of "first thing tomorrow" was somewhat different than Esther's.

We were about to give up and go in when a blue truck turned into the parking lot. The closer it came (and it didn't come closer very fast), the more I decided it was less blue and more gray. By the time it rolled up to the curb, I realized it had been constructed from trucks that had been blue, green, and black.

Esther popped out of the bed before it had finished rolling. "David, you got my message!"

"And who am I, no one?" Spencer asked.

Esther didn't answer, just grabbed whatever they were hauling. "I have the—poster here," she said between noisy gasps for breath. "But I'll admit—it's kind of—heavy."

I crinkled my nose. "How can a poster be heavy?"

Before she could reply, a man with a rosebush for a beard climbed out of the driver's seat and grabbed the other end. As he helped her lug it toward the tailgate, I caught my first glimpse of the poster. It looked shiny.

Esther dusted off her hands. "I stayed up all night to finish it. Toby helped, of course."

"Who's Toby?" I replied.

Esther motioned toward the man. "You know the guy who owns Renfro's?" Her chest puffed up with pride. "Well, that's Toby, my stepdad."

The man with the rosebush beard saluted, but he didn't bother to reply. But then, Mr. Renfro had never struck me as a man of many words. He was into modern art, which, according to Dad, meant that he built toilets out of scrap metal, then put them on display. He had a studio on State Street, but no one had ever bothered to go in until he'd turned it into an ice cream parlor, too. Now Renfro's was the hottest—or maybe the coldest—spot in town.

Esther slapped him on the back. "He even taught me how to weld!"

I had no idea what welding was, but it obviously excited Esther (and since Esther was an artist, having a stepdad like Mr. Renfro must have been a pretty sweet deal). But as they turned the poster toward us, I couldn't help but shake my head. It was made of tons of mirrors in a hundred different shapes and sizes.

Esther hopped down from the truck bed. "Now, I know what you're thinking—there's no freaking *way* we made this for fifty bucks."

"Actually," Spencer muttered, "I was wondering what the heck it—"

"Yeah," I interrupted as I jabbed him in the ribs. "That's *exactly* what we're thinking."

Esther dusted off her hands again. "Well, you don't need to worry. Toby and I picked this up as scrap. The guy at the hardware store was gonna chuck it, so we offered to take it off his hands, and he said we could just have it!"

"Wow," was all I said. For once, I'd been rendered almost speechless. And like Spencer, I couldn't figure out what the heck it was.

"I know, right?" Esther said as she grabbed one of the edges and swung it around for us to see. "So what do you think?"

I didn't answer right away, just dug my toe into a crack. Now that I could see the whole thing all at once, I had to admit it was impressive. The sun had just crested the peaks of the mountains that cradled

SV, and the mirrors seemed to catch every one of those pink rays. But I still had no idea what it was supposed to be.

I raised a hand to shield my eyes as I tried to figure out how to break the news to Esther. But I didn't have a chance to come up with the words before Riley's eyes widened.

"It's David," he said softly.

I crinkled my nose. "What is that supposed to mean?"

Riley pointed at the poster.

I tilted my head to the side, trying to see it how he saw it. And just like that, I did. That top mirror was my head, and the smaller bits stuck to my face were my eyes, my nose, my mouth. A set of trapezoids made up my torso, and four cascades of rectangles made up my arms and legs. Connecting wires ran through the whole structure to give the poster three dimensions, so a hundred reflections of my face could stare back at me at once.

Spencer wasn't impressed. "But what is it supposed to *mean*?"

"It means he's a part of us," Riley said. "And we're a part of him."

"Like the Blob?" Spencer replied.

Esther shook her head. "No, like a metaphor," she

said. "When other kids look at this poster, I want them to see themselves."

I was catching the vision, but Spencer still wasn't convinced.

"It doesn't say his name," he said.

Esther rolled her eyes. "It doesn't have to say his name. David's the only other candidate in the race."

Spencer shook his head. "As the campaign manager, I'm telling you that it has to say his name."

He faced her, and she faced him, putting herself between him and the poster. It was like we'd traveled back in time to a dusty street in a cardboard town. I started whistling the theme song for *The Good, the Bad and the Ugly*, but when someone fired up a lawnmower, the engine drowned me out.

Esther stuck out her chin. "You're not touching Shiny David."

Spencer snorted. "Shiny David?"

"That's his name," Esther replied. "And he's more than a poster. He's a work of art."

He opened his mouth to argue, but before he could get the words out, I threw myself between them.

"If the name is so important, then we'll add a sign," I said.

Spencer's forehead furrowed. "But what will it say?"

We set our sights on Riley, who was our designated speechwriter and official slogan maker-upper. He puckered his lips and folded his arms across his chest. I was familiar with that look, but he usually only got it when he was writing in his notebook.

We just stood there waiting as the sun's belly appeared, casting the mountains' craggy faces in a checkerboard of lights and darks. The lawnmower smelled like gasoline but also grass clippings, my second favorite smell. I drew a deep breath through my nose, but before I could release it, Riley's lips un-puckered.

"I have it," he said breathlessly, then raced into the school.

NINE

W E MOUNTED SHINY DAVID on the wall outside the lunchroom. Esther had brought a roll
of Velcro tape (which was surprisingly sturdy stuff).
Spencer even liked the placement. Connecting my
campaign to French fries was good subliminal adver-
tising in his book.

And of course, there was the sign.

"Your Face, Your Vote," it said in Esther's spidery
handwriting. We'd had no choice but to write it on
the back of an old math assignment, but Riley's words
still rang with authority. It was the best thing he'd
ever written, even better than his last slogan, "This
Grainger Ain't No Stranger."

Between classes, we camped out in the alcove down
the hall from Shiny David so we could watch other
kids discover him. They would stare for a few seconds, their faces scrunched up in confusion, and then
everything would click, and they would poke their

friends and random strangers and whisper excitedly. We couldn't hear what they were saying, but we had good imaginations:

It's amazing!

It's incredible!

Do you think Esther designed it?

Okay, so maybe she was the only one who thought they were saying *that*.

By the time lunch rolled around, kids had smacked me on the shoulder so many times that I'd lost track, so to avoid the teeming hordes, I opted to enter through the side door. I skirted the edges of the lunchroom, keeping my eyes trained on the ground. I'd never had to work so hard to be invisible before. And I was working so hard to be invisible that I didn't notice Esther, who was sitting at our table, until I almost sat on her.

I clutched my lunch box like a shield. "What are you doing here?" I blurted.

Esther didn't answer, just stuck her chin out at my lunch box. It wasn't until I looked down that I remembered it was Teenage Mutant Ninja Turtles day.

"My favorite's Donatello," Esther said.

Slowly, I lowered my shield. "You're a TMNT fan?" I asked.

"I guess," she said dismissively, "but I was referring

to the artist. He was a sculptor, too, you know. His most famous piece was *David*."

"Don't you mean Shiny David?" Spencer asked.

"No, I meant *David*," she replied, "as in the kid with the slingshot." She glanced at me, then at my seat. "Were you gonna sit down?"

"I don't know," I admitted. I wasn't really comfortable eating lunch with girls. I'd picked up some bad habits from my youngest older brother, Owen (who ate food like he fixed cars—with his mouth hanging open and his tongue lolling out the side). But I didn't want Esther to think that I wasn't grateful, either.

"Look, I don't like this situation any more than you do," she replied, "but if you want to win this race, then you have to count me in." She flicked a thumb over her shoulder. "Did you really think *your* posters were gonna get you any votes?"

"Well, at first, we thought they might," I said, "but then we saw Veronica's and knew that we were sunk."

She took a swig of chocolate milk. "It was a rhetorical question."

I crinkled my nose. "What does 'rhetorical' mean?" For some reason, it hadn't come up in any of Mom and Dad's old law books.

She shook her head. "Never mind."

Luckily, Spencer arrived before I could dig the hole any deeper. His hands were full of milk straws, and his eyes were wide and sparkling. "Guys!" he said, breathing hard.

Esther punched him in the arm. "I'm here, too, you know," she said.

The fact that Spencer didn't punch her back went to show just how pumped he was. "They love it, they absolutely love it!"

I figured *it* meant Shiny David, but I wasn't sure who *they* were. "Who loves it?" I replied.

"Everyone!" he said, then shook his head. "Okay, maybe not everyone. But some of them, at least, and some is way better than none!"

Riley fished another carrot stick out of his lunch tote. I'd tried to let him borrow one of mine, but apparently, his mom didn't believe in un-recycled plastic. The lunch tote was made of old milk jugs and, according to the label, wouldn't spend the next millennium leaching chemicals into a landfill. That was a good thing, but then, it *did* look like a diaper, so I guess there were always trade-offs.

"What are you talking about?" he asked.

"I took a straw poll!" Spencer said.

"What's a straw poll?" I replied.

"I don't know," he admitted. "But they're always talking about them on CNN, so that must mean they're important."

Esther lobbed a French fry at his head. "Well, if you don't know what it is, then how could you take one, doofus?"

The French fry hit him in the eye, but he managed to ignore it. "I took my own straw poll," he said. "I stood at the end of the lunch line and gave everyone a straw, but before I gave them one, I asked who they were gonna vote for."

Anxiety tap-danced in my stomach. "I appreciate the thought, but the rules say we can't hand things out…"

"Not even milk straws?" Spencer asked.

"Not even milk straws," Esther said, lobbing another French fry at his head. "And isn't it your job to keep track of things like rules?"

This time, Spencer dodged it. "Look, I don't need some airhead artist telling me how to do my job."

She drew herself up to her full height. "Well, unfortunately, this *airhead artist* is the only one getting things done!"

"That's not fair," Spencer replied, taking a swig of her chocolate milk. "I did the straw poll, didn't I?"

She folded her arms across her waist. "So what did they say?" she asked.

He wiped his mouth off with his sleeve. "Most said that they'll vote for Veronica." When Esther tried to interrupt, he held up a hand to stop her. "But *twelve* people told me that they were gonna vote for David."

My heart had started thumping, but as soon as he said "twelve," I felt my chest slowly deflate. We'd been plodding through the public school system since we were in kindergarten, so our class size hadn't changed since the Johnston twins had moved away. The last time I checked, we'd numbered a hundred and fifty-three.

"Twelve?" Esther asked. "That's it?"

Spencer scowled. "Hey, twelve is awesome! That's twelve more votes than we had yesterday."

"No thanks to you," she muttered.

Spencer managed not to comment. "And tomorrow, it will be twelve more, and the day after that, we'll get twelve more, until we have every vote from every kid and Ms. Quintero names you president and we give Veronica the boot." He slapped me on the back. "It's all downhill from here, David. It's all downhill from here."

Riley snorted. "Not likely."

I wasn't sure who to believe.

TEN

BY THE END OF seventh period, I was ready for a break. My cheeks were sore from smiling, and my shoulders were black and blue from getting thumped and bumped all day. If it had been up to me, I might have called it quits right then. The MMM had gotten me into this mess, and the MMM could get me out. But when I got to the office, she was nowhere to be found. I was about to turn around when I heard what sounded like raised voices.

I'd never given student council much more than a passing thought, but I managed to remember that they met with Ms. Quintero once a month. They were supposed to air our grievances, but I'd heard they spent their time sucking up to Ms. Quintero and binging on pizza and breadsticks. So much for representation.

On any other day, I would have hightailed it out of there, but my feet were tired, too, and I'd be lying if I said I wasn't curious. I leaned back against the door and folded my arms across my chest. The voices were coming from the conference room, so there was zero chance that they would see me, but if someone came along, I was going to need a good excuse to be hanging out around the office. Since I didn't have a phone, I'd have to pretend to be asleep.

"—would be a change," a voice was saying. It sounded like Veronica's. "But I think it would be nice to mix things up, try something new."

Someone snorted. "Don't be stupid." This voice sounded like Brady's. "We're only having this conversation because that twerp entered the race. But it's not going to matter, since he's just going to lose."

I was less concerned with this assessment than the fact that he'd called me a twerp. No one except my older brothers ever got to call me *that*.

"It's not just that," she said. "I mean, how would you feel if you never got a chance to make your opinions known?"

"It's a good question," someone said. I didn't recognize this voice. "But there are other ways. We don't have to let them have our seats."

Veronica drew a bracing breath, then slowly blew it out again. "I know I'm asking for a lot, but if it's for the greater good…"

Brady snorted again. "What good is it to suck up to a bunch of nerds?"

I had to bite my lip to keep from snorting myself. Was Veronica really suggesting that the populars step down so the nerds could take their seats?

There was an awkward pause, and then Ms. Quintero said, "I think that's all we have time for today. We'll have to take this up next month. Thank you, Ms. Pritchard-Pratt, for your thoughtful presentation. You've given us a lot to think about."

They weren't the only ones. But I didn't have a chance to process it before they descended on me.

I made a break for the south hall, but I'd never been the strongest runner, so I wasn't out of sight before Veronica called after me, "Hey, David, wait up!"

Waiting for Veronica wasn't high on my to-do list, but her unexpected cheerfulness took me by surprise. It sounded as fake as Granddad's dentures, and I'd never thought of her as someone who had to fake anything.

By the time I turned around, she'd already halved the distance between us. "We need to practice," she announced.

I opened my mouth to answer, then snapped it shut again. Brady had come up behind her and was now glaring lasers at me, like I was some kind of amoeba that had latched onto his shoe. It might have had something to do with the tail end of that meeting, but I'd never thought of him as someone who cared about that stuff.

Veronica knocked on my forehead. "Earth to David, Earth to David!" When I blinked, she said again, "We need to practice, like, right now."

I tore my gaze away from Brady's face. "Yeah, sure," I said distractedly. Maybe Brady thought that I was trying to make a move on his girlfriend. Nothing could be further from the truth. "Why don't we plan on tomorrow?"

She grabbed the handle on my backpack. "Why don't we plan on right now? Can I come over to your place?"

"His place?" Brady asked. He asked it like my place was one of those toxic waste facilities that belched green smoke into the air.

She made a show of shrugging. "We've practiced at his house before."

I fought the urge to smack my forehead. If he'd been worried before, Brady had to be downright suspicious now. "Only once," I said, backpedaling, but Veronica wouldn't let me go. I must have looked like a cartoon character that couldn't run away.

Veronica didn't seem to notice. "So are we going?" she demanded.

I shifted awkwardly. On the one hand, I wanted to play "La Vie en rose" with her again, but on the other, it seemed stupid—and possibly life-threatening—to incur Brady's wrath. The last thing I needed was a vengeful boyfriend on my tail.

I was trying to decide how to let Veronica down gently when I remembered my saving grace. "Well, my parents are downtown, and they don't let me have friends over when I'm home alone."

Brady stuck his chin out. "Who said you two were friends?" he asked.

"Well, they don't let me have enemies over when I'm home alone, either, so it's kind of a moot point."

Brady smiled smugly. "Then I guess we'll just have to postpone—"

"Do you want to come over to my house?" Veronica cut in.

"WHAT?" Brady replied. "You've never asked me over, and we've been going out for months!"

She held up a hand to stop him, then set her sights on me. "Do you or don't you?" she demanded, folding her arms across her waist.

I dug my toe into the carpet. I *did* want to play "La

Vie en rose," and if I was being completely honest, I also wanted to see her place. If Brady hadn't been there, it must have been a sight to see. They probably had security checkpoints, maybe even an electric fence. Her house was probably the nicest of any of the houses in SV.

"I'd have to call my mom," I said.

Veronica motioned toward the office. "I bet you can use their phone. They let me use it all the time."

"Don't you have your own?" I asked.

"It's a secure line," Brady said. "You know, like a president's."

Veronica actually blushed, but she didn't disagree. That must have meant that it was true.

Still, I hesitated. "I'd also have to see if she could pick me up."

Veronica relaxed. "Even if she can't," she said, "I could help you catch the bus."

Brady straightened up. "So can I come over, too? I've never seen your—"

"No, you can't." The way that Veronica said it left zero room for argument. "David and I will have to practice. We won't have time for official tours."

Worry sizzled in my stomach like an egg in a hot pan. No Brady meant no witnesses. Was this some clever ploy designed to lure me to her lair?

I chuckled nervously. "Your parents aren't ax murderers, are they?"

"Of course not," she replied (though she refused to meet my gaze). "It's just that…never mind. I guess you'll see soon enough."

Since she was still clutching my backpack, it wasn't difficult for her to drag me back into the office. Brady sputtered like a dying engine, then, finally, stormed off. I couldn't help but wonder if he'd gotten the better deal.

As I dialed Mom's number, a part of me secretly hoped she'd put the kibosh on this whole plan, but she thought it was a grand idea. She felt like she knew everyone (since she'd been on the school board in Radcliff's day), but she couldn't know Ms. Pritchard or Mr. Pratt—could she?

Veronica lived on the last street of her school bus's last stop. I'd expected that school bus to take us up into the foothills that overlooked the valley, but when it turned west instead, I realized that I'd been off. *Way* off. By the time we clambered down the steps, we'd clattered over the train tracks and left the paved roads far behind. The houses on this side of SV were set apart by several acres, probably to accommodate the farms that had once been so common. But no one farmed anymore, so now it looked like the west-siders were trying to avoid their neighbors.

She kept up a running commentary as we tromped up the street. "That's Old Lady Foster's place," she said as she pointed at a house with a rusted-out Volkswagen Beetle. "She's Evelyn's grandma, though Evelyn would never admit it."

Evelyn Schmidt had been a popular through most of elementary school, but I'd heard that she and Veronica had had an argument. Evelyn and her closest friends had stopped sitting with the populars, but since she was the head cheerleader, we still thought of her as one.

"And that's the Markhams'," she went on, pointing at a clapboard shack. "They don't really go outside, so their place looks worse than it is."

It certainly couldn't look much worse.

"And that's the Laras'," she continued. She didn't comment on their house, since we were coming up on hers. "And this...well, this is mine."

It wasn't the worst house on the street—that honor went to the Markhams' shack—but that wasn't saying much. The yellow paint was old and faded (where it hadn't peeled off completely), and the whole house sagged to the left side. One corner of the porch had given out, and it looked like someone had put a baseball through a window and never bothered to replace it. They'd put a board up, though. The duct tape was a nice touch.

She drew a bracing breath. "Nowhere to go but in," she said.

I had no choice but to follow.

The living room lived up to the outside, with ragged curtains and curling wallpaper. The whole place smelled like cigarettes. Or at least I thought that smell was cigarettes. I guess I didn't really know.

Veronica crinkled her nose. "I apologize about the smell. I know your parents probably don't—"

"What about the smell?" a voice cut in.

We turned toward it in unison. A beautiful woman had popped up in the archway that connected the front room to the house. Her long, blond hair looked like Veronica's (though it did look slightly crunchier), but her alligator business suit looked nothing like the ones that were stuffed at the back of Mom's closet. It clung to her like plastic wrap, and it wouldn't have surprised me if the alligator had turned out to be real.

Veronica just shook her head. "Nothing, Mom. Forget I said it."

I'd already decided that the woman was her mom,

but I didn't like the way that Ms. Pritchard was looking at me—like I was a piece of meat.

"Well, hello there," she said smoothly as she sashayed
into the room. "What's your name, little one?"

I wanted to tell her I was Radcliff—for some reason,
it seemed dangerous to tell her who I was—but the lie
caught in my throat. "My name is David," I replied.

She offered me her hand. "And mine is Sue," she
said, winking.

I shook Ms. Pritchard's hand as quickly as I could.
"Nice to meet you," I mumbled. Though I called
Riley's parents Beau and Abigail, it felt weird to call
her Sue.

Ms. Pritchard tipped her head back and cackled
like I'd just said something funny. I cocked an eyebrow at Veronica, but she didn't seem to know what
her mom was laughing at, either.

"You'll have to clear out now," she said as she
rushed her mom away. "David and I are going to
practice, and I know how much you hate the noise."

Ms. Pritchard stood her ground. "Well, maybe I
could listen just this—"

"No!"

Veronica's outburst took me by surprise (and if I
didn't miss my guess, it took Veronica by surprise,

too). But instead of backing down, she drew herself up to her full height. I couldn't help but notice that she had her mom by several inches.

Ms. Pritchard made a show of sniffing. "I can see when I'm not wanted." She flipped her hair over her shoulder. "But I expect you to make dinner as soon as David leaves!"

Ms. Pritchard stormed off in a huff. When a door slammed shut upstairs, I jumped despite myself, but Veronica deflated.

"I apologize about her, too," she said. "My mom is kind of…"

"Loud?" I finished.

She half snorted, half sighed. "Dad keeps saying he'll divorce her, but Mom knows that he's too chicken—and that we need the health insurance. She works at Kaufmann Travel, but I'm pretty sure she spends more time at the hair salon next door. When Mr. Kaufmann's gone, at least." She glanced down at her All Stars. "But that was way more information than you probably needed."

I forced a nervous chuckle. I wasn't used to worrying about things like health insurance (or what Mom did to stay busy), so I didn't know how to relate.

"Anyway," she said as she lifted the piano lid, "we

should get started. I don't know how long I'll have." She glanced back at the archway, then returned her attention to the keys. "How about some warm-up scales?"

"Sure," I said, shrugging, not because I liked warm-up scales—I didn't—but because I needed a second to adjust. For some reason, it hadn't occurred to me that Veronica's life wouldn't be perfect, that it wouldn't be like mine.

ELEVEN

VERONICA DIDN'T MENTION "La Vie en rose" for the rest of the week, but that was fine by me. I didn't want to be her confidante or even her friend. And with the campaign at a standstill, I had plenty on my plate.

Spencer was on the verge of tears when he got to lunch on Friday. "Five," he said dejectedly. I wasn't sure if he was talking about the straws still in his hand or the ones he'd given away. "Kepler, only five!"

Esther, who'd managed to make herself a regular fixture at our table, retrieved one of the castoff straws. "Only five *what*?" she asked.

"Only five people told me that they were gonna vote for David, and Sarah Sloan said she'd change her mind if I didn't stop bothering her."

Riley perked up. "Sarah Sloan?" He'd had a crush on her forever.

Spencer waved that off. "It doesn't matter who it

was! The numbers are what matter, and they've been dropping like my uncle's stock."

Spencer had taken straw polls at every lunch this week, and the news wasn't encouraging. I'd scored thirty straws on Wednesday (which he'd attributed to Shiny David), but the numbers had been falling ever since. Today's count was a new low.

I scratched the back of my head. "You know, maybe Sarah's right. Maybe we just need to take a break."

Spencer shook his head. "It's not just that," he said, sighing. "The campaign is losing steam. We need to do something, and quick."

Esther drained her chocolate milk, then slammed the empty carton down. "I'll take care of it," she said, "and I'll do it quickly, too."

Spencer's eyes narrowed. "You've got something up your sleeve?"

"Can't say I do," Esther replied, holding out her arms to prove it. Then she pointed at her head. "But I've got plenty of ideas up here."

"What kinds of ideas?" I asked.

Her only answer was a wicked grin.

I spent the afternoon waiting and wondering, but Esther didn't disappoint. Between sixth and seventh periods, she magically showed up at my locker with a stack of postcard-sized flyers. She tried to hand them to me, but Spencer intercepted them. After giving them a once-over, he handed them to me. I had to squint to read Esther's spidery handwriting:

Meet us behind Renfro's
at exactly 9:00 a.m. tomorrow for
THE EXPERIENCE OF A LIFETIME.

Spencer made a face. "What's 'the experience of a lifetime'?"

"And why at Renfro's?" I added.

"You'll see," Esther replied, still smiling like the Cheshire Cat. "For now, just pass these out."

The color drained from Riley's cheeks. "We're supposed to give them to just anyone?"

"No, to *everyone*," she said, handing us a few more flyers. "We want everyone to be there. We want everyone to own this."

"Own *what*?" Spencer demanded.

"The experience of a lifetime," she said simply. She turned around, then turned right back. "And you can come without a shirt. It'll just get in the way."

As much as it shamed me to admit it, I almost peed my pants right then.

✳ ✳ ✳

Riley and I showed up at Spencer's house at eight thirty the next morning. It was only a few blocks from Renfro's, so it had seemed like a good meeting place. He met us on the porch, his bare chest gleaming in the sun. We didn't bother to say anything, just dipped our heads at one another. If we were going to go down, at least we would go down together.

The walk to Renfro's was a short one, and since we were coming at it from behind, we could see Esther hard at work long before we actually got there. She was sitting on a crate, leaning against Renfro's back wall, a funnel perched between her legs. A water balloon dangled from the end, though she wasn't filling it with water. The multicolored streaks that stained her arms looked suspiciously like paint.

When Spencer kicked a rock that skittered across the empty lot and eventually stopped next to her crate, Esther looked up from her funnel. "Hey, guys!" she said, waving. Flecks of paint went flying, landing in her curly hair, but she didn't seem to notice. "I'm glad you decided to come early."

"What are you doing?" Spencer asked, planting both hands on his hips.

DON'T VOTE FOR ME

Esther looked him up and down. It made me glad I'd brought a shirt. "What do you think?" she replied as she tied off the balloon. "We're gonna do a little painting!"

Unease rumbled in my stomach like an approaching thunderstorm, but I managed to ignore it. "So what are we gonna paint?"

Her grin might have been contagious if it hadn't been so terrifying. "I'll give you one guess," she replied as she retrieved a T-shirt from a grocery sack and chucked it in my direction. "Here, put this on."

I caught the T-shirt in both hands, then bobbled it and finally dropped it. When I picked it up again, it had a dirt stain on the back. "I got this one dirty," I said lamely, holding it back out to her. "And you forgot to take the tags off."

Esther took it back and snapped the tags off with her teeth, then tossed it back to me. "It doesn't matter," she replied, tossing shirts to Riley and Spencer. "They're about to get much dirtier."

That probably should have worried me, but I was more concerned about taking off my shirt. The thought of changing while she watched was enough to make me blush.

I dug my toe into the dirt. "Hey, Esther, would you mind?"

"Would I mind *what*?" she asked.

I felt my cheeks get hot. "Would you mind turning around?"

She sighed and rolled her eyes, but at least she turned around.

As soon as she turned her back, I shucked off my Care Bear shirt—another hand-me-down from Radcliff—while Riley did the same.

Esther made a show of cleaning paint out of her nails. "You know that I couldn't care less about seeing your chest, right?"

"All the same," I said, shoving my arms into the sleeves, "I appreciate the privacy." After yanking it over my head, I mumbled, "You can turn around."

"See, that wasn't so hard," she said.

I pointed at the masking tape that she'd stuck across the shirt. "What is this stuff for?" I asked.

"It's protecting the logo," she explained, peeling the tape back to reveal the first word of YOUR PAINT, YOUR VOTE.

Spencer peeled his tape away. "What if the paint bleeds underneath it?"

She considered that, then shrugged. "If it's just a few drips, it won't be a big deal. The paintballs are oil-based—otherwise, the paint would just wash off—so if the logo takes a hit, we would definitely be in trouble. But the tape is heavy-duty—it's the kind that Toby uses—so I think it will hold." She smacked Spencer's chest, hard. "Just don't fiddle with it, genius."

He made a face at her.

She pretended not to notice. "So this is how it's gonna work. When everyone gets here, we're gonna line up over there." She motioned toward Renfro's back wall. "Then we're gonna arm everyone with paintball guns and let them take potshots at us."

I crinkled my nose. "What do you mean, 'let them take potshots at us'?" I glanced at the wall, then back at Esther's paintball gun. "Oh, you mean they're gonna…?"

"Yep," Esther said, grinning. "And it's gonna be freaking amazing. Every time they see these shirts, they're gonna remember this moment."

I eyed the paint, the guns, the grocery sacks stuffed with new T-shirts. "This only cost you fifty bucks?"

"Well, the guns belong to Toby—he's part of this paintball league—but the rest of this stuff only cost me forty-seven eighty-three." Esther smiled proudly. "And I have the receipts to prove it."

I rolled my tongue around my mouth, but I was already out of spit. I guess it really was possible to be scared spitless.

"Don't worry," Esther said. "The first shot's always the toughest. After a while, you'll get used to it." She smacked me on the shoulder. "Let's get ready for battle!"

Riley checked his watch (which I sincerely hoped was paint-proof). "It's eight fifty-nine," he said.

Spencer pointed out two lonely figures headed up the street. "And here they come!" he crowed.

My heart lifted a little. I could handle only two. But what started as a trickle quickly turned into a stream, then a genuine deluge. By ten minutes after nine, the empty lot behind Renfro's was filled to overflowing with a sea of eager sixth graders. A few looked vaguely interested, but most looked downright eager to shoot us with paintball guns. They must have deciphered Esther's flyers a lot more quickly than I had.

Spencer climbed up on a crate. "All right, all right!" he said to get everyone's attention. "First off, we want to thank you guys for coming. Our art director—"

"That's me!" Esther said.

"—will explain how this will work," he said as if she hadn't cut in.

Esther cleared her throat. "All right, listen up!" she hollered. "This is pretty self-explanatory. We have these shirts, we have this paint, and we need you guys to help us put the two together."

One of the kids who was standing near the front—I thought his name was Jason—motioned toward the paintball guns. "Are we allowed to go for head shots?"

Esther sized him up. "Sure," she finally said, "if you think that you can hit one."

While everyone else snickered, I started composing my last will and testament in my head.

"In addition to the guns," she said, "we also have these paint balloons, so feel free to mix it up. And we have quite a few shirts, so even when we finish these"— she gestured to the shirts that we were wearing—"we'll have more to go around." She pointed at the kid who'd asked the question about head shots. "Jayden, I'm putting you in charge of giving everyone a turn."

Jayden nodded eagerly. Apparently, his name wasn't Jason.

"All right, then," Esther said. "Once we get our headgear on, we'll get to work!"

Esther's mention of headgear produced a couple of friendly boos, but the others seemed okay with it (and thank goodness for *that*). She handed each of us a fencing mask—or what I figured was a fencing mask—and showed us how to put it on. I was grateful for the mesh screen, since I didn't want anyone to see me when I accidentally squealed.

"We'll start with our backs," she said, pulling her mask over her face. "And please make sure you stay behind the solid yellow line!"

I snuck a peek over my shoulder. I hadn't noticed any line. With any luck, that meant it was on the *other* side of Renfro's.

Even though it was only nine, the wall was already warm. It was a good thing we had the masks, since my nose probably would have scraped it. I wanted to sink into that wall and grab a root beer float at Renfro's (or, better yet, escape when the others weren't looking). I fought the urge to barf as the crowd shifted behind us. Jayden must have been organizing everyone into a line and distributing the ammo.

Too soon, he shouted, "Fire!"

I'd never actually fired a paintball gun before, but Owen and Radcliff had both owned one, so I knew that creepy hissing sound wasn't a good sign. You had to attach compressed air canisters to make paintball guns fire, so they let off little hisses every time you squeezed the trigger. But I only had a second to think these less-than-helpful thoughts before a dozen welts rose on my back. I had to bite my lip to keep from screaming.

"Next!" Jayden shouted firmly, and there was a momentary lull as the weaponry changed hands.

I pressed my mask against the cinderblock and waited for that telltale hiss. The second volley missed our shirts, but somehow, it found our legs. As more welts bloomed on my calves, I cursed myself for wearing shorts.

While Jayden helped the next group, I blinked back nervous tears. A sudden breeze blew through the empty lot, stirring the leg hairs that weren't already plastered with paint. The breeze smelled like ice cream sundaes, and for a second, maybe more, I actually felt kind of good. So when the next wave of ammo hit and one of Esther's paint balloons exploded on my head, I did something unexpected:

I actually laughed out loud.

The sound bubbled up my throat before I could tell what it was. It started as a snicker, then morphed into an all-out belly laugh, knocking me onto my knees. By the time I got back up, Spencer was belly-laughing, too, and even Riley had stopped whimpering. We must have looked insane.

Esther, who'd been grinning like an idiot from the moment we'd arrived, slapped me on my paint-streaked back. "See, it's not so bad," she said.

I was laughing too hard to reply.

She slapped me on the back again. "I think it's time to turn around!"

Hysterical tears clouded my vision, so even after I turned around, I couldn't tell what was going on. When a nervous hush descended, I rubbed the tears out of my eyes. The crowd was parting around something like a school of fish around a shark, and even though the something—or, more precisely, the some*one*—was still a long way from the front, I could tell who the shark was.

Apparently, Veronica had come to play with her food.

TWELVE

By the time Veronica reached the yellow line, the crowd had gone perfectly still. They were probably too afraid to speak, or maybe they just wanted to hear our bones break when she snapped us in half.

"David," Veronica said as she dipped her head at me.

I was still wearing the mask, so how she knew which one was me, I honestly had no idea. "Hi," was all I said. My voice echoed in my ears, sounding small and insignificant.

As her entourage fanned out behind her, I couldn't help but notice there was one of them for one of us. Brady had lined up across from Esther, and Hector and Samantha were trying to out-glare Riley and Spencer.

Hector exposed his teeth in a rough approximation of a grin. "Looks like you're having a fiesta."

Esther's hands clenched into fists. "Well, no one invited *you*."

"Really?" Hector replied, pulling a flyer from his pocket. "Then how did we end up with this?"

Esther ripped her mask off. "Where in Shepherd's Vale did you get that?"

"Wouldn't you like to know?" he asked.

I squinted at the flyer. It was smudged with pencil lead (and what looked like carrot juice).

I set my sights on Riley. "Why'd you give *them* one?" I asked.

Riley held his hands up. "I didn't!" he insisted. But then he ducked his head. "But I did throw some away."

Esther's face flushed purple. "You were supposed to pass them out!"

"I had extras," Riley said.

"You weren't supposed to *have* extras," I replied.

Veronica motioned toward the flyer. "So anyone can take a shot?"

I snuck a peek at Esther (who was sneaking a peek at me). "That was the idea," I said slowly.

Veronica stuck out her chin. "Then we want to take ours."

Our eyes met, and somehow, an unspoken agreement passed between us. I knew that she was baiting me, waiting to see if I would blink. Owen and Radcliff had been fond of playing chicken with the beaters that had always accumulated behind Classics by Jesse (though they'd sworn me to secrecy, since Mom would have freaked out if she'd known), but these stakes seemed so much higher.

I swallowed, hard. "All right." I wouldn't be the first to blink.

Spencer pointed at the back. "But you'll have to wait your turn."

Jayden had just handed her the gun, so he tried to take it back.

Veronica didn't let it go. "Do you really want to make me wait?"

Now it was my turn to rip my mask off. If she wanted to go toe to toe, we'd do it face to face. "Of course not," I replied. I hoped I sounded braver than I felt. "We want you to take your turns and go."

Veronica cocked an eyebrow. It looked like she was smiling, sort of, but it was probably an illusion. "Don't you want to put your mask back on?"

I wasn't sure if it was bravery or just plain, old stupidity, but if I put that mask back on, I knew I wouldn't win a single vote. So instead of doing the right thing, I drew myself up to my full height. "No, Veronica, I don't."

A shudder rippled through the crowd, but Veronica just shrugged.

"Suit yourself," was all she said as she raised the paintball gun.

She was far enough away that I couldn't tell where she was aiming, but the one thing I did know was that it was going to hurt. I clenched my teeth and stared her down, and for a second, maybe less, I thought she smiled again.

The smile caught me off guard, and I almost relaxed. Maybe I'd been wrong. Maybe "La Vie en rose" had changed her as much as it had changed me. Maybe we were almost friends. But before I could decide, Veronica drew a bracing breath and calmly squeezed the trigger.

The paintballs hit me in the chest, one right after the other. I lost track of the number as they burst against the tape, exploding against my chest like blood bursting from a wound. I stepped back to catch myself, but I didn't find my balance. I found Spencer's rock instead. It caught my heel and tipped me over, and as I staggered back against Renfro's, the paint—red paint, I noticed—dribbled down into the dirt and collected into gleaming beads.

Esther dropped to her knees beside me, cushioning my fall. She put a hand behind my head, which would have made an awesome death scene if I'd actually been dying.

I guess Spencer didn't get the memo, because he launched himself at Veronica. "Holy Faraday, you killed him!"

Before Spencer could make contact, Hector caught him by the wrist, taking him down in one smooth move. "Don't be an idiot, *muchacho*."

Spencer fell flat on his face, but he didn't let that stop him. He looked like a dying worm as he writhed and squirmed in place, pinned down by Hector's claw-like grip. He definitely wasn't giving up, but he wasn't gaining any traction, either.

His back glistened with wet paint, and his front must have been a mess, but Samantha didn't seem to mind. After planting herself on his back, she growled, "Stop that, or we'll kill you next."

Spencer finally stopped, but whether he'd taken her threat seriously or he could no longer move, I honestly couldn't have said.

"Say something," Esther croaked, brushing the hair out of my eyes.

I looked down at my chest, which was still dripping with red paint, then slowly, very slowly, tugged at a corner of the tape. A bead of paint bled down the front. YOUR PAINT, YOUR VOTE, it said, and now that paint was Veronica's.

I managed a weak smile. "That's gonna look amazing when it dries."

Esther's gaze darted back and forth between my face and the T-shirt. Finally, she grinned. "Yeah, I guess it will," she said as she held out her hand. "Way to sacrifice yourself."

I took hold of her hand, and she towed me to my feet. As I surveyed the scene, the other kids hollered and catcalled—but not the populars. Hector sneered, Samantha spat, and Brady made a face. Veronica, on the other hand, just returned the gun to Jayden, then slowly turned around.

The crowd gave her a wide berth as she strutted off into the sunset (or, in this case, the sunrise). I squinted at her back, grateful that she couldn't watch me watching her, but just before she turned the corner, she snuck a peek over her shoulder.

"Nice shirt," was all she said.

Esther's experience of a lifetime had turned into a celebration by the time they disappeared, but instead of joining in, I sat down on a crate and tried to puzzle out her words.

THIRTEEN

THE T-SHIRTS WERE A hit. Making them had been epically awesome—my arms and legs were still covered with paint—but what made the whole thing even better was that they were also cool. Spencer couldn't have been happier. He wanted to hand them out like candy, but Esther and I agreed that that would be against the rules, so Spencer did the next best thing—he signed them out like library books.

Esther tried to argue that that was still against the rules, but Spencer wouldn't listen. On Monday, YOUR PAINT, YOUR VOTE T-shirts descended on the school like locusts. Though there were only twelve of them, they seemed to pop up everywhere: on the bus, in Mr. Ashton's class, on the way to lunch. Spencer probably had the schedule down to the class period.

As soon as he got to the table, Esther pushed her lunch aside. "So?" she asked. "How many straws?"

He couldn't do much more than grin.

Esther punched him in the shoulder. "Are you gonna say something, or are you just gonna sit there giggling?"

He drew an overdue breath. "Thirty-eight!" he finally squeaked.

I looked down at my lunch box to disguise my goofy grin. Thirty-eight was nowhere near enough, but it was a heck of a lot better than five.

Spencer yanked a Milky Way out of his pocket and held it up over his head. "And next week, it will be fifty-eight!" He took a bite of Milky Way, then looked this way and that. "But have you guys heard the rumors?"

"What rumors?" Esther asked.

Spencer licked his lips. "I heard the queen bee fought with her drones."

A shiver skittered down my spine—somehow, I knew where this was headed—but before I could react, Esther actually squealed.

"About what?" she demanded.

"Well," Spencer said slowly, obviously enjoying the attention, "word on the street is that Veronica suggested that they integrate at the last student council meeting. She thought more 'geeks and dorks'"—he made air quotes with his fingers—"should get a chance to hold a spot."

I shifted uneasily. The only reason they were rumors instead of verified facts was because no one had talked to me.

"And *then*," Spencer went on, "she dumped Brady in a fit of rage when he wouldn't back her up."

I shook my head. "She didn't dump him."

Three pairs of eyes zoomed in on me, and I realized what I'd just said. I would have smacked my forehead if it wouldn't have made me look guiltier.

"Well," I said, backpedaling, "I meant that she *couldn't* have dumped him. We saw them on Saturday, remember?"

Esther shook her head. "Just because they were together doesn't mean they're still *together*."

"Oh," was all I said.

While Spencer and Esther went on speculating about Brady and Veronica's relationship, I went back to my lunch. Why had I opened my big mouth? It never turned out very well.

I was halfway through my sandwich—PB and bananas for the win—when someone tapped me on the shoulder. "David Grainger?" a voice asked.

Hesitantly, I turned around. A perfect-looking girl was standing right behind me.

"Are you David?" she asked again.

Instead of answering, I nodded.

The girl didn't seem surprised. "The principal would like to see you."

I hugged my lunch box to my chest. "Right now?" I'd never had to go to the principal's before.

The girl half nodded, half frowned. "I'm afraid so," was all she said.

I could have made a run for it, but something told me that this girl, with her long legs and killer ponytail, would have run me down in a second. Grudgingly, I rose to my feet, but before I could climb over the bench, Spencer grabbed me by the arm.

"David can't come right now," he said, biting off a chunk of Milky Way. "We're kind of busy at the moment."

"I'm sorry," the girl said (though she didn't sound very sorry), "but Ms. Quintero said it couldn't wait."

I wriggled out of Spencer's grip. "What is this about?" I asked.

"Your campaign," the girl said, blinking.

Spencer stuck himself between us. "Then you have to take me, too. I'm his campaign manager, you know."

The girl shrugged. "I don't care. Just as long as David comes." And with that, she spun around, obviously expecting to be followed.

Even though the girl had made it sound like Ms.

Quintero would be waiting for us, she made us sit in a pair of plastic chairs for another hour, give or take. When the MMM finally waved us in, I could barely stand up straight (though that might have had something do with my wildly trembling knees). My pudding cup clunked around my lunch box, a grim reminder that I hadn't finished. I probably could have eaten it, but I'd been too wound up to swallow.

Spencer and I paused on the threshold of Ms. Quintero's office. She was spraying down her desk with a fine mist of disinfecting spray while she talked to Ms. Clementi (who was shamelessly pinching her nose). It made the whole place smell like soapy lemons, but I guess that smell was better than whatever twelve-year-olds smelled like.

They'd been deep in conversation, but as soon as they spotted us, they stopped and waved us in. I tried to act casual, but my toe caught on the strip that divided the industrial-grade carpet from the slightly less worn-out linoleum, pitching me into her office like a badly thrown baseball. At least I managed to land in one of the chairs in front of her desk.

"Have a seat," Ms. Quintero said. Apparently, she hadn't noticed that I was already sitting. "We'll be with you in a moment."

"What are we waiting for?" I asked at the same time a familiar voice piped up, "What does this have to do with me?"

I couldn't help but wonder what it had to do with Veronica, too. Now not only did I get to have my very first nervous breakdown, but I got to have it in front of *her*. I guess class presidents weren't forced to wait in plastic chairs.

"Quite a bit, unfortunately," Ms. Quintero said.

Veronica sank into the seat that was closest to the door.

Spencer sat down in the other one. "What's going on?" he asked.

Ms. Quintero didn't answer until she'd wiped off the disinfecting spray and pulled a paper from her desk. "It has come to my attention that an unauthorized school function was held on Saturday, May seventh. I've also been informed that you surpassed the spending limit set forth in the school constitution and that you handed out T-shirts in violation of the rules."

No sooner had the word "violation" left her mouth than Spencer leaned across my lap to glare malevolently at her. "Did you tell them?" he demanded.

Veronica's eyes glinted. "Of course I didn't," she replied, but then she set her sights on me. "Seriously, David, I didn't tell them."

If I hadn't known better, I might have thought that my opinion mattered.

Ms. Quintero raised a hand. "Mr. Chen, please let me finish."

"No, you let *me* finish," he said. "We didn't give those shirts away, we only let kids borrow them. And Esther promised us she didn't spend more than fifty bucks."

Ms. Quintero sighed. "Does that mean that you're admitting you held an unauthorized school function?"

It wasn't like we could deny it. Though it had been more than two days, we were still covered with the evidence.

Luckily, Spencer didn't try to. "We didn't mean to," he replied. "That's got to count for something, right?"

Ms. Quintero didn't answer, just turned her attention to me. "Well, Mr. Grainger?" she demanded. "What do you have to say for yourself?"

Instead of answering, I swallowed, hard. It felt like I'd just eaten a dozen PB and banana sandwiches and couldn't get my mouth unstuck. And even though the weatherman hadn't said a word about the pollen count, my eyes were suddenly watering. What was happening to me?

Ms. Clementi had been strangely silent, but my sudden-onset hay fever must have made her take pity on me. "It's all right, David," she said. "If you confess your crimes right now, we'll only duct-tape you to the dodgeball mats for the next twenty-four hours."

Or maybe it hadn't.

Ms. Quintero gasped. "Cara!"

Ms. Clementi waited, then threw her head back and cackled like the Wicked Witch of the West. "Hyperbole!" she said.

Veronica and I didn't react, but Spencer choked on his own spit.

Ms. Quintero cleared her throat. "I think what she's *trying* to say is that the consequences of your actions will be infinitely less severe if you don't try to drag this out." She folded her arms across her desk and fixed me with her Care Bear Glare.

I looked back and forth between them, wiping tears out of my ears. Ms. Clementi was still giggling, but Ms. Quintero looked especially grim. She claimed she didn't like to punish us—she only did it for our own good—and for once, I almost believed her.

I snuck a peek at Spencer (who was trying to melt into the floor), then let my gaze slide to Veronica (who was inspecting a hangnail). If she was trying to ignore me, she was doing a first-rate job. But when I looked away, she glanced at me, and when I glanced at her, she looked away. For some reason, that gave me the courage to say what I needed to say.

I drew a shaky breath. "What Spencer said is true. We didn't mean to break the rules. The other kids don't get the T-shirts, they only get to borrow them. And the paint and everything only cost forty-seven eighty-three. Our art director—her name's Esther—said she kept all her receipts, but more than that, she doesn't lie."

The words were pouring out of me even more quickly than usual, but instead of spiraling out of control, they fit together like a puzzle. For the first time in my life, my mouth was actually working with my brain.

"As for the experience of a lifetime"—I wiped my hands off on my jeans—"we didn't think that it would count as an unauthorized school function. Esther only thought it would be a cool way to make the shirts."

Ms. Quintero arched an eyebrow. "Are you saying that Ms. Lambert is responsible for these violations?"

"No!" I said, then cleared my throat. "I mean, no, Ms. Quintero. I'm not trying to blame anyone." I glanced down at my toes to give myself more time to think. "I'm the one running for class president, so I should be the one who accepts responsibility."

Ms. Quintero sighed, then dragged herself out of her seat. "You'll have to give us a few minutes."

While she and Ms. Clementi deliberated in the hall, I tried not to hyperventilate. Mom was going to kill me when she found out that I'd been summoned to Ms. Quintero's office (or, worse, she'd just enroll me in those miserable piano lessons).

I was still working on my breathing when Ms. Quintero came back in. "I appreciate your honesty, Mr. Grainger, and I especially appreciate your willingness to accept responsibility. I'm inclined to believe that your campaign didn't violate the spending limit, and I'm even willing to go along with the revolving distribution of these T-shirts." She pressed her lips into a line. "Nevertheless, the fact remains that you hosted a school function without obtaining anyone's permission, and I'm afraid the penalty for that is a week's worth of detention." She dropped her gaze, then added, "And no student serving detention is allowed to run for a class office."

"WHAT?" Spencer replied.

Ms. Quintero managed to ignore him. "I'm assigning you and your associates one week's worth of detention and officially suspending your campaign." She smiled sadly at Veronica. "I guess that makes you next year's seventh-grade class president. Congratulations, Ms. Pritchard-Pratt." She motioned toward the door. "You're welcome to go back to class."

More tears pricked my eyes, but I managed not to let my hay fever get the better of me. I'd take this news like a man if I had to bite my lip until it bled.

But Spencer wasn't so determined.

"You can't do that!" he replied, gripping both edges of his seat. "You can't just take it away!"

"I'm pretty sure she can," I mumbled. "And I'm pretty sure she just did."

Saying it out loud like that made it feel real for the first time, and with the realness came discouragement. I'd been wishy-washy from the start, but I guess a part of me had gotten into it, had finally started to believe.

"But it can't be over," Spencer peeped, dragging a hand under his nose. Either he'd caught a cold, or Riley was rubbing off on him.

I didn't have a chance to comfort him before Veronica raised her hand. "Excuse me," she replied, "but don't I have a say in this?"

Ms. Quintero blinked. "I guess you do."

She tossed her hair over her shoulder. "As far as I'm concerned, David and his paint brigade can serve detention for a year." She looked at me, then looked away. "But whatever you do, please don't make him quit the race."

FOURTEEN

I DUG MY FISTS INTO my ears. I must have misunderstood her. There was no other explanation.

"I'm sorry," Ms. Quintero said, "but I don't think I heard you right. Did you really say you *don't* want me to make Mr. Grainger quit?"

Veronica nodded. "Yes, I did."

Ms. Quintero shrugged. "If you really feel that strongly, I suppose an exception could be made. Mr. Grainger *has* already shown that he can be quite honest when he wants to be." She started to pull out her disinfecting spray, then realized what she was doing and promptly closed her desk again. "That will be all for now, children. Ms. Clementi will arrange the details of your detention."

"Come along!" Ms. Clementi said as she herded us out of the room.

After Ms. Clementi made us swear that we'd show up for detention on pain of ripping out our nose hairs,

Spencer released a held-in breath. "Well, that could have gone much better, but it also could have gone much worse." He shoved his hands into his pockets. "I guess this means I'll see you later?"

I nodded tiredly. "Right after seventh period."

Spencer motioned toward Veronica, who'd just moseyed out behind us, apparently not in any hurry. "Don't let her give you any crap."

After Spencer wandered off, I sent her a sideways glance. "Are you following me?" I asked.

"Well, of course I am," she said. "There's only one way out of the office."

I felt my cheeks get hot. "Oh, right."

"But since you're here," she hurried on, "I was thinking we could show Mr. Ashton what we've got."

I honestly hadn't seen this coming. I hadn't thought about "La Vie en rose" for what felt like forever. "Yeah, sure," I said uncertainly. "You can talk to Mr. Ashton."

"I already did," she said. "He's expecting us to be here at seven thirty in the morning."

I swallowed, hard. "All right." I hadn't thought that it would be so soon, but I could make it work. "I guess I'll see you then."

Veronica nodded toward my shirt. "It turned out all right, don't you think?"

I glanced down at my chest. I'd forgotten I was wearing my YOUR PAINT, YOUR VOTE T-shirt. When Esther had handed me this one—the one Veronica had tagged—I hadn't bothered to object. Ending up with this T-shirt had seemed like a foregone conclusion.

"I guess," I said, rubbing my chest. I didn't see a reason to reveal how much I secretly liked it. "If you don't mind all the bruises."

"It didn't hurt *that* bad," she said.

"And how would you know?" I replied.

"Because I've played paintball before."

I opened my mouth to answer, then snapped it shut again. I was surprised that she'd played paintball (but I guess that would explain how she'd shot me so efficiently).

"Besides," Veronica continued, flicking a piece of lint off her shoulder, "paintball guns are child's play."

I knotted my arms across my chest. "Does that mean you've shot something more powerful?" I seriously doubted it.

"No, but Hector has."

That took me by surprise. "Does his family hunt or something?"

She paused, then shook her head. "He's from East Los Angeles, you know."

What that had to do with anything, I couldn't have said. "So why'd he move?" I asked.

"You'll have to ask him that," she said.

I crinkled my nose. "Like *that's* ever gonna happen."

"All right, then, ask your mom."

"My mom?" I asked, surprised. "What does this have to do with her?"

Veronica didn't reply, just shook her head again and headed off the other way.

✳ ✳ ✳

The next morning, Mom drove me to school for my meeting with Veronica. She'd been driving me a lot lately, and the truth was, I liked it. Most moms were dull or awkward, but mine was easy to talk to.

Except when I couldn't decide whether or not I wanted to talk.

Unfortunately, nothing got past Mom. After making a right turn, she casually motioned toward my legs. "Do you have ants in your pants?"

"No," I said. "Well, yes." But that probably wasn't true. I quickly checked under my legs. "Well, not literally, I guess."

She pinched me on the cheek and tucked some hair

behind my ear. This might have been a safety hazard if we'd been doing more than twenty-six. She never drove fast anymore—she said she was cashing in the minutes she'd banked from living life in the fast lane—but I had a hard time believing that she'd ever cracked thirty.

I leaned against the window. "It's just something someone said." I sent her a sideways glance. "Have you ever heard of Hector Villalobos?"

Mom accidentally punched the gas pedal. "Maybe," she admitted after we'd slowed back down to twenty-two. "What have *you* heard about Hector?"

"Just that you knew him," I replied.

When we got to the next stop sign, she shifted the gearshift into park. She'd always been a careful driver, but this was *too* careful, if you asked me. "I don't know Hector," she replied, "but I do know *of* him. He has the same name as his granddad, who I knew in California."

"You knew his *granddad*?" I replied.

"In case you haven't noticed," she said, smiling, "your dad and I are older than most of your friends' parents."

I'd never thought about it quite like that, but I guess it was true enough. Riley's parents were as old as Elias and his wife.

I tried to connect the dots. "So Hector lived in California?" When she nodded, I muttered, "He was probably in a gang."

"That's an awful thing to say," Mom said, then glanced down at her lap. "But in this case, you'd be right."

I didn't like the sound of that.

"You have to understand that this was years ago," she said before I could interrupt. "I'd just passed the bar exam, so I hadn't accepted the position with McGrath and Moody yet. For those first few years, I worked for the Central District Court, and in the first month, they appointed me as Hector's granddad's counsel."

I knew that Mom had been a lawyer, but it was weird to hear these details. She'd never mentioned any of this stuff (but then, I'd never asked).

"I did my best," she said, "but I was green, and he was Mexican. The trial was over almost as soon as it began. They found him guilty of three counts of possession and another two counts of assault—one of which was aggravated—which came to twenty years in prison."

I crinkled my nose. "Ouch."

Mom nodded absently. "Three strikes, and you're

out—or *in*, as the case may be. Hector didn't stand a chance." She looked down at her lap again. "Somewhere along the way, he decided that he wanted out."

"Out of prison?" I replied.

Mom shook her head. "Out of his gang. I don't know how he did it, but when he walked out of state prison, he rounded up his kids and grandkids and somehow made a run for it. Luckily, his friends never caught up." She half chuckled, half sighed. "I guess he'd had a lot of time to plan."

I tried to imagine sneaking out in the middle of the night, constantly looking over my shoulder, wondering if Granddad's friends or enemies were going to knife me while I slept. But the image wouldn't settle. That was a movie, not real life.

But it had been Hector's real life once.

"One day," Mom went on, "I got a call out of the blue. It was Hector, of course. He wanted—needed—a safe place where he could watch his grandkids grow, and I immediately thought of Shepherd's Vale. They moved in a few months later." She glanced at me across the cup holders. "You probably don't remember that, do you?"

I wanted to tell her that I did, that I remembered Hector's first day at school, but I couldn't bring myself to lie, not about something this important. Carefully, I shook my head.

Mom considered that, then shrugged. "I always wondered if you two would get along, but I guess you don't have a lot in common." She tilted her head to the side. "Does Hector have friends of his own?"

Instead of answering, I nodded. He had more friends than he could count. But what I'd never considered was that I could have been one of them.

Thanks to our little chat, I was ten minutes late to school (or at least ten minutes later than I'd expected to be). My trumpet case banged against my knees as I galloped down the hall. It occurred to me that my legs might get tangled up with my trumpet case just before they did just that.

I grunted when I hit the ground, but I was more annoyed than hurt. The hall was mostly empty—a few art kids were hanging out around Mr. Nelson's room, but I didn't think they'd noticed me—so at least I hadn't made a scene. Still, I stayed down for a second so I had time to catch my breath, but what I ended up catching were the haunting strains of a piano. They started soft and low, but then the notes slowly crescendoed until they filled the whole south hall. It was the most beautiful thing I'd ever heard.

I scrambled to my feet and followed the notes down the south hall. It was only when I reached the door to Mr. Ashton's room that I realized what I was hearing.

The room was empty except for *her*. She was playing without music, and the only light was seeping through the still-closed blinds. Her eyes were closed, and she was swaying like a piece of barely anchored seaweed. Okay, maybe not like seaweed, since seaweed was kind of gross, but like something light and free.

She went on for a while, until I couldn't have said how long I'd been standing there, five minutes or five years. Then the music stopped abruptly. When I opened my eyes—I hadn't noticed that I'd closed them—it felt like I'd just woken up from a deep, untroubled sleep.

"You stopped," was all I said.

"I didn't think anyone was listening."

"What *was* that?" I replied, scrubbing the sleep out of my eyes.

"'Nocturne in E Flat Major.'" She shoved the bench out of the way. It screeched on the linoleum, dispelling the last traces of magic. "It was written by Frédéric Chopin."

I motioned toward the piano. "Why don't you just play that?"

"It doesn't have a trumpet part," she said.

I waved that away. "Who cares? You can play it by yourself."

"I can't play something by myself," she said.

I crinkled my nose. "Why not?"

"Because my parents wouldn't get it. They think music is a waste. It can't dig a ditch or make a casserole or book someone else's five-star cruise." She kicked the back of the piano. "It's only good for idiots who want to go to schools like Lietz House."

Thanks to Mr. Ashton, I'd heard of Lietz House before. He might have been unreasonably obsessed with pastries, but he knew a lot about music, so it was probably a decent school. Why wouldn't they want her to attend?

"My dad moved to Shepherd's Vale halfway through his senior year," she said. "His last name was Pratt, so he ended up in Mom's homeroom—in the desk in front of hers, in fact. She flirted with him like she cared, and he fell for her so hard that he actually proposed on the day they graduated." She glanced down at her toes. "By the time he figured out that she flirted with everyone, she was already pregnant."

I had no idea what to say or how to say it, so I didn't say a word.

She must not have known what to say, either, because she grabbed her messenger and made a beeline for the door. "Out of my way," she growled.

Obediently, I got out of her way.

"If Mr. Ashton ever gets here, let him know I couldn't stay."

I looked around the room. "Why not?"

"Because I can't let someone catch me hanging out around the band room." She glanced at me over her shoulder. "I don't want anyone to talk."

It was less of a statement than a warning. She was the queen bee of the populars, but she was an imposter—and I was the only one who knew. For some reason, she'd decided to let me in on her secrets, so if anyone found out, it would be my fault. That was a heavy load to bear alone.

She tossed her hair over her shoulder, but before she could get away, I asked, "If your parents don't like music, where did you get the piano?"

She'd been about to turn the corner, but my question made her stop. "I stole it," she replied.

My eyes bulged. "You did *what*?"

"I stole it," she said again, but this time, she smiled wickedly. "From that old lady down the street. You remember her place, don't you?"

I managed a weak nod. Radcliff had been involved in petty crime, but the most that he and Michael had ever managed to get away with was a pair of pink flamingos from Mr. Seltzer's yard (and those flamingos hardly counted, since Mr. Seltzer was mostly blind).

"I'd tell you how I did it," she went on, "but that information's classified." With one last grin, she added, "I hope you have a nice day."

FIFTEEN

I SPENT THE REST OF the day wondering about that darn piano. I should have asked a million questions: *How did you know that it was there? Why did you turn to common thievery? How did you get in—and more importantly, how did you get out?* Pianos weren't exactly portable.

By the time that I got home, my head was crammed with questions, but my parents were too busy tangoing to take the time to answer them. There were several problems with this picture, but the biggest one was that my parents didn't know how to tango. Dad looked like a scarecrow with his gangly arms and legs, but Mom didn't seem to care. She was giggling like a schoolgirl and letting Dad drag her around. Not even the grease under his nails seemed to bug her in the least.

They tended to forget that they still had a kid at home whose reputation, such as it was, would be ruined forever if anyone from school ever caught a glimpse of them.

I cowered behind the Challenger, trying to decide how to cut in (or if I even wanted to). But before I could make my mind up, Mom caught a glimpse of me.

"Well, hello, David," she said as Dad tipped her over backward. "Did you have a nice time in detention?"

She'd been flaming mad when she found out (which was just as I'd predicted), so this was probably her way of making me feel like a dolt.

If she was waiting for me to collapse, she was going to be disappointed. "It was fantastic," I replied with as much excitement as I could muster. Actually, we'd spent the whole time stapling packets, so it had been as dull as a PBS documentary.

She and Dad swooped past his tool chest, narrowly missing the screwdriver that hadn't quite been put away, but when he tried to twirl her, she twirled herself away.

"Is something wrong?" she asked, tucking some hair behind my ear.

I motioned toward Dad's stereo. "Do either of you know Frédéric Chopin's 'Nocturne in E Flat Major'?"

"Do I know it?" Dad replied, tossing his rag onto

his workbench. It was like he'd just been waiting for me to mention good old Frédéric. "That's like asking Albert Einstein if he knows quantum physics!"

I dug my toe into a crack. Though I'd heard of Albert Einstein, my education hadn't covered any of the stuff he'd actually done. "Does that mean you've heard of it?"

Instead of answering, Dad pulled the remote out of his coveralls and aimed it at the stereo. It didn't take long for the notes to sound familiar. The pianist on the recording easily could have been Veronica.

Dad slipped the remote back into his coveralls. Whether they had pockets or just really deep folds, I couldn't have said. "Where did *you* hear it?" he asked. "I didn't think he wrote for bands."

"He didn't," I replied. "I heard about him from Veronica. Or I heard her play his piece."

Dad nodded knowingly. "And how did it sound?" he asked.

"It sounded *great*," I said, remembering how the notes had scratched an itch I hadn't even known I'd had. "I mean, it sounded kind of sad, but it was a really pretty sad." The recording hit those thirty-second notes, and I couldn't help but sigh. "But when I suggested that she play it instead of 'La Vie en rose,' she just blew me off."

Now it was Mom's turn to nod knowingly. "Why do you think she did that?"

I considered that, then shrugged. "She said her parents don't like music, but who doesn't like music?" I squinted up at them. "And why wouldn't they want her to go to Lietz House?"

Mom and Dad exchanged a weighty look. It could mean all kinds of things, but in this case, it probably meant, *Do we think he's old enough to discuss big, scary things like music schools?* I was really sick of being the only minor in the family.

Finally, Mom patted my back. "It would be great if she could play it, but maybe now isn't the time."

"When will it be the time?" I asked.

"I don't know, David. Maybe never." She patted my back again. "But even if the time is never right, you can always be her friend."

I made a face. "But she's a popular. We're as different as PB and bananas."

She tilted her head to the side. "I think you and Veronica have a lot more in common than you think."

"Like what?" I asked, incredulous.

"Like Trash to Treasure," Mom replied.

Dad nudged my trumpet case toward me. "And don't forget 'La Vie en rose.'"

I retreated to my room so I could sort everything out, and the more I thought about it, the more I decided that Mom and Dad were right (again). No one else from school ever went to Trash to Treasure, and Veronica and I were probably the only two kids on the planet who'd ever heard of Edith Piaf. Then it occurred to me that Veronica might have thought I'd told her to play the nocturne because I didn't want to play "La Vie en rose," but that wasn't it at all.

If I'd kept these thoughts to myself, I probably would have been all right, but when I made the mistake of sharing some of them with Mom, she completely freaked out. Instead of asking me questions like a normal human being, she stuffed my trumpet case and me into the back of the mini-van (since I still didn't weigh enough to sit in the passenger seat). I tried to convince her to let me call Veronica instead, but she wouldn't hear of it. Apparently, there were some apologies that you had to make in person.

We took a few wrong turns past the train tracks, but when I spotted the old Beetle hanging out on the corner, I knew we'd found the right street. The mini-van's new tires crunched over the sun-choked weeds as we pulled into her driveway. I'd always wished that

Mom and Dad had splurged on a Lamborghini (or at least a Cadillac), but for once, I was grateful that they drove a beat-up Honda Odyssey. Compared to the Beetle, the Odyssey was the height of luxury.

Mom checked the address, then announced, "Well, it looks like this is it."

I didn't bother to confirm it, just tightened my grip on my trumpet case.

Mom nipped me on the nose (which, for once, I didn't mind), then threw the gearshift into reverse. "Call me when you're finished."

I felt my pulse speed up. "I thought you were gonna wait."

"Not this time," Mom replied. "Some things you have to do alone."

I glanced up and down the street. Just like the last time I'd been here, there was no one to be seen, but the dry weeds shivering in the wind seemed like an especially bad omen. "But what if something happens?"

"Nothing's going to happen," she replied, then cupped my cheek and smiled sadly. "This isn't East Los Angeles."

I drew a bracing breath. If Hector could leave everything he'd ever known behind, then I could get out of this car. I grabbed hold of the latch, then gently popped open the door. For some reason, it seemed hotter than it had last week.

"Call me!" Mom said again. When she started to pull away, I had no choice but to close the door.

I waited until the minivan disappeared, then forced myself to climb the steps. That second-story window still had a baseball-shaped hole, and the sagging porch still looked like it was about to collapse. I didn't have a chance to knock before someone yanked the door open—and the someone wasn't Veronica.

Mr. Pratt ducked under the lintel to get a better look at me. "What is it?" he demanded, propping his arm against the door.

I caught a whiff of dirt and sweat, but I forced myself to hold my ground. He might have been intimidating, but it was probably going to be worse if he thought I was a wimp.

I snuck a peek under his arm. "Is Veronica around?"

"Why do you want to know?" he asked, squinting at me through red-rimmed eyes. "And who are you, anyway?"

I thought about sticking out my hand, then changed my mind at the last second. "My name is David Grainger. I think we met at Trash to Treasure."

His frown morphed into a scowl. "Oh, yeah, I

remember you. You're Mr. Basketball." He glanced over his shoulder. "Can you believe that, Ronny? This kid thought I could play!"

I kept my eyes trained on his work boots (which were coated with fresh mud). "Only because you're tall," I said. "I mean, what are you, seven feet? You must have eaten a lot of broccoli—unless those broccoli rumors are a lie. I've always thought they were. Adults will say just about anything to get kids to eat their vegetables."

Mr. Pratt wrinkled his nose. "Do you always talk this much?"

"Only when I think someone might pound me through the pavement."

No sooner had the words "pound me through the pavement" left my lips than I knew that I'd said the wrong thing. The next ten seconds of silence were the longest of my life. I fully expected Mr. Pratt to pull out his trusty mallet and make good on my threat, but he clapped me on the back instead.

"I think I like you, kid," he said (though his grip said quite the opposite). "Why don't you come inside?"

He dragged me into the living room by the scruff of the Ford T-shirt I'd inherited from Owen, then kicked the door shut on my heels. One of the seams on my shirt ripped, but Mr. Pratt didn't seem to notice, or maybe he just didn't care. At least he set me down again before it split completely open.

"You've got company," he told Veronica. "And I think he's here to make some noise."

She didn't get up from the couch. "What are you doing here?" she asked.

I tapped my trumpet case (though I couldn't bring myself to meet her eyes). "I just thought it would be nice if we could give our song a spin."

"Your song?" Mr. Pratt replied, glaring lasers at Veronica. "You and this boy have a song?"

"It isn't like that," she replied, her eyes as wide as two fried eggs.

"That's right," I said, nodding ferociously. "It's not our song at all."

"Then whose song is it?" he demanded.

We didn't have a chance to answer before the door flew open again and admitted Ms. Pritchard. Her hair was sticking out at crazy angles, and her pink lipstick was smeared.

"Is there a party going on?" she asked as she glanced around the room. When she got to me, she stopped—and smiled. "Well, hello again."

Veronica's cheeks turned the same color as Ms.

Pritchard's glossy lipstick. "We're kind of busy, Mom," she said.

"Oh, right." Ms. Pritchard winked. As she staggered down the hall, she shouted, "Have a good time, Ronny!"

Mr. Pratt gritted his teeth, but Ms. Pritchard didn't seem to notice. She disappeared without a backward glance, completely oblivious to what was going down in the middle of her living room. Mom never would have walked away from anything that looked like a fight.

Mr. Pratt glared at Veronica. "Your mother might not care about what's going on out here, but that doesn't mean I don't, so you'd better come clean *now*."

Veronica held up her hands. "It's really nothing," she replied. "We just got asked to play this song."

Mr. Pratt's eyes narrowed. "Play a song for *what*?" he asked.

Veronica looked down at her toes. "For the spring recital," she admitted.

Most parents would have offered Mr. Ashton all the bear claws he could eat if he would let their kid play a song, but Mr. Pratt wasn't most parents. I could tell that he was furious from the way he clenched and unclenched his fists. Veronica had never come to school with bruises, but I'd never really paid attention.

I was looking for a place to hide when Mr. Pratt managed to surprise me. He didn't explode, just knotted his arms across his chest. "I thought we both agreed this class was supposed to be for fun." He pointed his chin at the piano. "I thought we both agreed that music isn't worth your time."

"You said it wasn't worth my time," she said, "but I never agreed."

Mr. Pratt swore under his breath. "How many times do I have to tell you, Ronny, that the Pratts don't make big plans? We take what the universe gives us and find a way to live with it."

Veronica dragged herself up off the couch. "What if I don't want to live with it?"

"You don't have a choice," he said.

"Yes, I do," Veronica replied, drawing herself up to her full height. "Because I'm not just a Pratt."

Mr. Pratt rocked back on his heels like his daughter had just struck him (and in a way, I guess she had), but she didn't take it back. I expected him to strike her back, but he didn't raise his fists. He didn't even raise his voice.

"Yeah, well, you act like a Pritchard a little more every day," he said.

Before Veronica could answer, her dad stormed off

in a huff. A few seconds later, one of the upstairs doors slammed shut.

She held it together for a moment, then collapsed onto the couch and pressed her face into her hands. As her shoulders shook with silent sobs, I prayed that someone, *anyone*, would beam me out of this tight spot, but no one came to my rescue.

I guess that meant that maybe I was supposed to come to hers.

"I'm sorry," I whispered. It didn't seem significant enough, but it was the best that I could do. "If I'd known he didn't know—"

"It's not your fault," she interrupted. "I should have told him a long time ago." She dragged a hand under her nose. "I should have told him everything."

The way she said "everything" connected the dots in my head. "Is that why you do what you do, the music and the sports and student council—so you can get into that magnet school?"

She didn't answer right away, just glanced down at her vintage All Stars. I thought her cheeks turned pink, but since she was no longer looking at me, it was hard to say for sure. When she clicked her heels together, it made me think of Dorothy, but apparently, her All Stars weren't as powerful as ruby slippers, because she was still stuck in this house, this life.

"I do some of it for Lietz House," she admitted, running a hand down the piano. Her fingers traced the keys as lightly as they would a sparrow's wings. "But I do the music for me."

SIXTEEN

By the time Mom came back, I was ready to run away, waving my arms over my head. Veronica was a decent human being (which scared me more than I cared to admit), and maybe, just maybe, she needed to win this race more than I did.

Still, I shuddered at the thought of trying to break this news to Spencer. He'd probably lecture me for days (and that was only if he didn't pants me and run my boxers up the flagpole). So when he called an impromptu meeting in the middle of detention, I slouched down in my seat and tried not to catch his eye.

Officially, this meeting was for Riley, who was supposed to be writing my speech, but we all knew it was for Spencer, who liked playing campaign manager a little too much, if you asked me. I would have felt safer if Ms. Clementi hadn't left, but as soon as we'd arrived, she'd yanked her staple gun out of her desk and made a beeline for the door, mumbling something about bullet—or bulletin—boards. Either way, she'd disappeared, leaving us alone with Spencer, who wasn't wasting any time.

"Forty-one!" he crowed as he pulled a straw out of his pocket.

"That's not that many," Riley said. I had no choice but to agree. Forty-one out of a hundred and fifty-three wasn't going to win any elections.

But maybe that was a good thing.

Spencer rolled his eyes. "Well, I didn't ask *every-one*," he said.

Esther straightened up. "So how many did you ask?"

"I don't know," Spencer replied. "Fifty or sixty... or a hundred."

"Forty-one out of a hundred is a heck of a lot worse than forty-one out of fifty," Esther said.

Spencer waved that off. "It doesn't have to be exact. That's why they call it a straw poll." He returned the straw to his pocket. "But the numbers are definitely climbing. I'd say this calls for a toast!"

Now it was Esther's turn to roll her eyes. "You can't toast without a drink."

Spencer produced a chocolate milk out of nowhere. He must have gotten it at lunch, which made it at least three hours old. "To David!" he went on as if she hadn't interrupted. "We've run an excellent campaign."

Esther made a face. "And what am I, a slug?" she asked.

"And to Esther!" Spencer added as he downed a healthy swig. When he didn't even flinch, I couldn't help but be impressed. "You've had some excellent ideas."

At least that seemed to appease her. But Riley, who'd been scribbling busily for the last several minutes, didn't even look up from his notebook.

Esther tried to catch his eye. "Don't you want a toast?" she asked. When Riley didn't answer, she craned her neck to see his notebook. "I said, don't you want a toast? The least you could do is answer me. The speech can't be *that* interesting."

Spencer and I had gotten used to the way that Riley could zone out when he was tinkering with something new—he'd once spent a whole episode of *The Legend of Korra* perfecting his "Ode to a Carrot Stick"—but Esther clearly hadn't. When she tried to grab his notebook, he snatched it back with feisty hands, pressing it against his chest.

Spencer downed his chocolate milk. "If he's acting that cagey, he can't be working on the speech."

Spencer's grin turned menacing. "I bet he's writing love letters instead."

The tips of Riley's ears burned red, and I shifted awkwardly. Riley had had a crush on Sarah Sloan since the end of the first grade, when she helped him to his feet after he'd tripped into the shallow end at SV's annual swimming party. The truth was, he'd almost drowned, but we never talked about it, and now Spencer was discussing it in front of a real, live girl.

I expected Riley to faint dead away, but when he snapped his notebook shut and dragged a hand under his nose, I knew that it would be much worse.

"At least I don't pretend to hate someone I'm actually in love with." His gaze flickered to Esther. "So why don't you just kiss her and get it over with already?"

Spencer's eyes widened, then narrowed. Riley arched an eyebrow. My hands started to sweat, since it seemed like bloodshed was imminent. I snuck a peek at Esther, but she was tightening her shoelaces, so I couldn't read her face. I would have been tightening mine, too, if I was going to need to make a break for it.

Spencer stuck his chin out. "All right, then, maybe I will!"

Riley motioned toward Esther. "All right, then, be my guest!"

That knocked Spencer back a step, but he managed not to lose his balance. After leveling one last glare at Riley, he turned his attention to Esther. She looked up just in time to see Spencer coming toward her with his lips partially puckered. She leaped out of her seat and scrambled back against the counter. Ms. Clementi's Kleenex box collection, which extended nearly to the ceiling, promptly cascaded to the floor.

"What are you doing?" Esther screeched.

"Something I should have done two weeks ago."

"What does *that* mean?" she replied as her eyes darted back and forth between Riley, Spencer, and me. "Would someone please explain what in Shepherd's Vale he's doing?"

Riley just sat there smiling as Spencer advanced on her position. I tried to look away, but a part of me wanted to see if he would actually go through with it.

She must have sensed my hesitation. "David, what's going on? Tell me right now, or I'll pound you."

I opened my mouth to answer, then changed my mind at the last second. I doubted that she wanted to hear that Spencer was going to kiss her because Riley had dared him to.

Spencer planted himself in front of Esther. Guilt

and curiosity tugged at my insides. Was he really going to kiss her? And was I really going to watch?

Esther just stood there gaping, but whether she was too shocked or too grossed out to move, I couldn't have said. She had five inches on Spencer, but it looked like she'd forgotten. "David!" she finally shrieked. "Don't just sit there, do something!"

It was the shriek that did me in. Mom had been trying to civilize me, and despite my best efforts to resist *her* efforts, I couldn't deny that that shriek had gotten to me. No gentleman would stand idly by while Spencer accosted a young lady, so I did the first thing that popped into my often empty head:

"I want to quit!" I said. It came out as a hiccup, but at least it did the trick.

Spencer spun around. I couldn't help but notice that his cheeks were red and splotchy. "What did you just say?" he asked.

"You heard me," I replied, locking my wobbly knees. "I said, I want to quit."

Spencer dropped his arms. "You can't mean that," he replied.

Maybe I couldn't. I guess it was possible that I'd only said it to save Esther, but even as I thought it, I knew it wasn't really true.

"I do mean it," I said. "Absolutely."

"But why?" Esther demanded. She'd never cried in my presence, but it suddenly sounded like she was trying to hold back tears.

I scratched the back of my head. "I don't know," I admitted. "I guess a part of me just feels sorry. I mean, what if this election is more important than we think? Maybe she wants to *be* a politician." It was harder to tell lies when you knew what the truth was. "Or maybe she just cares about her future."

Esther's forehead crinkled. "What are you talking about?"

But Riley had already figured it out. "It's 'La Vie en rose,' isn't it? You fell in love with some dumb song, so now you think that you're in love with her."

"In love with *Veronica*?" I asked. I could honestly say that it hadn't crossed my mind. "I'm sorry to disappoint you, but Veronica isn't my type."

"Too popular?" Esther asked.

"No, too short," I replied.

That earned me a grin from Esther, but Riley was less than impressed.

"Well, if it isn't the song, then what is it?"

"I don't know," I said again. "You know, she's

really not that different. And what if she doesn't care about being class president or even being popular?"

Spencer crinkled his nose. "If she doesn't care about that stuff, then why does she bother?" he replied.

I made a show of shrugging. She hadn't exposed Hector's secrets, so I wouldn't expose hers. "Maybe she just does it for fun."

Spencer kneaded my shoulder. "I know this has been overwhelming and the spotlight's been kind of bright—"

"More like blistering," I muttered.

"—but the *point*," Spencer went on as if I hadn't cut in, "is that you're not just running for David Grainger anymore. You're running for every kid who's ever stopped and seen his face in Shiny David. And you're running for every kid at every school who's ever wanted to beat the populars. So are you really gonna let them down—not to mention let *us* down—and drop out of this race?"

I swallowed, hard. Spencer was great at guilt trips, and he did have a point. When you dressed it up like that, running for class president was the most worthwhile thing I'd ever done. It hadn't started out that way, but that was what it had turned into. And at least forty-one sixth graders in SV agreed.

"All right," I finally said, wriggling out of his grip. Just because I had to say it didn't mean I had to like it.

Spencer thumped me on the back. "That's what I want to hear!" he said. And with that, he marched back to the front, reassuming his position as designated campaign manager.

Spencer went on, of course, but I was no longer listening. This back-whacking had to be the toughest part of a campaign. It was too bad I'd said I'd stay.

SEVENTEEN

When I saw Veronica in band, I couldn't bring myself to meet her gaze. I was afraid that she'd see through me, that she'd somehow know I'd caved. I stared straight ahead instead, keeping my eyes on Mr. Ashton, but it nowhere near as easy to keep my thoughts on him, too.

We were halfway through "The Stars and Stripes Forever" when a man appeared in the doorway. He was slender and bespectacled, with a lonely tuft of silver hair in the middle of his head. He was also wearing a bow tie and a coat with elbow patches. I couldn't decide whether he looked more like a professor or an evil mastermind.

Curious, I lowered my trumpet. Then the others lowered theirs. I'd never had so much power over my classmates before, but then, maybe it was the man who'd drawn their attention on his own. He definitely looked out of place.

Finally, Mr. Ashton noticed, too. "Doug!" he boomed in welcome, and I couldn't help but crinkle my nose. The man didn't look like a Doug. "I'm so glad that you could make it."

The man glanced at his watch. "I believe you said nine thirty? It looks like I'm interrupting."

Mr. Ashton waved that off. "Get your workbooks out," he told us, "and go over the scales at the bottom of page sixty-two." Then he glanced in my—our— direction. "David, Veronica, come over here for a second!"

I honestly couldn't imagine what the man might want with me. College was still years away, and recent events had shown my evil-masterminding skills weren't exactly up to snuff.

As I climbed down the risers, I snuck a peek at Veronica. She was smoothing her shirt like she was about to meet Bruce Wayne. I glanced back at the man—maybe he was a superhero in disguise—but except for those suede elbow patches, nothing about the man stood out.

We followed Mr. Ashton out the door, where we found the man waiting patiently. He offered his hand to Mr. Ashton, but instead of shaking it, Mr. Ashton threw his arms around his shoulders. The man chuckled nervously, but it didn't look like Mr. Ashton noticed.

The man cleared his throat. "It's been a long time, James," he said with what sounded like an accent.

"Too long," Mr. Ashton said. "But I'm so glad you could come and meet my two rising stars!"

The man extended a pale hand. "I'm Douglas Lietz," he said. At least his real name wasn't Doug.

"Douglas *Lietz*?" I asked. That couldn't be a coincidence. I started to ask if the school was named after his family, but before I could get the words out, Veronica poked me, hard.

"It's a privilege to meet you, sir," she said. "We've heard great things about your school."

Mr. Lietz chuckled. He had one of those deep, pleasant laughs that reminded me of a bassoon. "And I've heard great things about your music." He motioned toward Mr. Ashton. "James here can't say enough about you."

I found that hard to believe. "What exactly has he said?"

"Only that he thinks you two are his most talented students." Mr. Lietz clicked his heels together. "Only that he thinks you may be Lietz House material."

Veronica blushed. "I can't believe you just said that."

Mr. Lietz smiled, revealing a row of slightly crooked teeth. They made him seem more authentic. "Believe it," he replied as he fished two fancy pamphlets out of his briefcase. "Lietz House may be small, but I believe you'll find we're worth considering."

I accepted the pamphlet and carefully turned it over. The paper was so textured that it made me think of the shirts I wore to church, and the pictures looked way too nice to be of a real place. I couldn't help but be impressed.

"I'm hoping to come to the recital," he went on, tucking his arms behind his back. "I understand that you'll be playing Edith Piaf's 'La Vie en rose'?"

"Actually," I said before Veronica could interrupt, "we were thinking about playing one of Frédéric Chopin's nocturnes."

She poked me again, harder. I tried to escape, but Mr. Lietz and Mr. Ashton had unintentionally boxed me in. It wouldn't have been so bad if I could have asked her what was wrong, but I wasn't about to have a heart-to-heart in front of other boys.

Mr. Lietz shifted uncomfortably. "I didn't realize they had a trumpet part."

"They *don't*," she growled, her nostrils flaring. "David here was only joking."

Her eyes dared me to deny it, but for once, I had the good sense to keep my mouth shut.

Mr. Lietz fixed his bow tie, and I got the impression that Lietz House students never joked. "Well," he replied with another nervous chuckle, "it was lovely to meet you." He retrieved his briefcase. "Until the recital?"

"Until the recital," she said, nodding. If she nodded any faster, her head was going to fall off.

I didn't bother to reply until Veronica stamped on my foot. "Yeah, sure," I said, wincing.

Mr. Lietz dipped his head, then headed back up the hall. We just stood there blinking until he disappeared around the corner, then exhaled in unison.

Mr. Ashton rubbed his jaw. "I guess that's what I get for letting David do the talking."

I hadn't meant to do *any* talking, but Veronica didn't let me explain.

"I need to use the hall pass," she announced, then whirled around and stalked away without waiting for his answer. The girls' bathroom was only a few doors down, so we were well within earshot when the door slammed shut behind her.

I winced instinctively. "I should go after her, shouldn't I?"

Mr. Ashton held his hands up. "Don't ask me,"

he replied. "I know even less about women than I do about sixth graders, and apparently, that's not much."

"I could have told you that," I said, then scurried off after Veronica.

EIGHTEEN

I SAT OUTSIDE THE BATHROOM for what felt like forever, hugging my knees against my chest like a snot-nosed kindergartner. I'd been praying to the bell gods for the last couple of minutes, but second period was still going strong. I couldn't decide whether that was better or worse.

I got so tired of just sitting there, staring blankly at the carpet, that I actually tried to count the stains, but I lost track around two hundred. Luckily, the squeak of rusty door hinges jerked me out of my trance. Veronica took one look at me and muttered, "For the love of Beethoven," then started to retreat into the bathroom.

But I hadn't been sitting out here for nothing. "Hey, wait!" I called after her as I lunged for the door.

Unfortunately, I didn't catch it before it closed on my fingers.

Now, some people might think your life flashed

before your eyes when you were on the brink of death, but it wasn't your whole life. It was just the stupid things you'd done, the mistakes you'd made along the way. As I slumped onto the floor, my fingers still caught in the crack, the only thing that I could think about was how I'd betrayed Veronica.

She ripped the door open again, mangling my fingers one more time. "Oh, David, I'm so sorry!" She fell to her knees beside me. "I didn't think you'd—"

"Don't say it." I cradled my hand against my chest. "I don't want anyone to think I was trying to sneak into the girls' bathroom. The last thing I need right now is a political scandal."

Veronica pursed her lips. "Will you let me look at your fingers?"

Slowly, very slowly, I extended my right hand. My middle fingers felt like broken twigs, and the few bits of skin and meat that hadn't been ground to a pulp were already starting to swell.

I swayed woozily. "That would look really cool if those weren't *my* fingers," I said.

"Come on," Veronica replied, dragging me up by my armpits. "We've got to get you to the nurse's office."

I let my arms go limp. "No, I want to stay right here."

"David," she replied, sounding dangerously like a mom, "we don't have any time to waste."

"No," I said again, wriggling out of her grip, "*we* don't need to do anything. We're not friends, remember? We're mortal enemies."

My fingers throbbed with every heartbeat, but at the back of my mind, those words pulsed like a beacon: *We're not friends, we're not friends.* If we *were* friends, we wouldn't be here. I would have dropped out of the race (or I wouldn't have entered in the first place).

Veronica rolled her eyes. "Don't be ridiculous, David."

"I'm not being ridiculous," I said as blood dripped onto my jeans. It seemed like too much blood for a couple of measly fingers. "I wanted to quit, I really did, but that old Spencer wouldn't let me. He said I wasn't just running for myself anymore. He said I had to think about everyone who was depending on me. He said I had to beat you."

It looked like she couldn't decide whether to smile or frown at this news. I wanted to ask her why—and why my fingers felt like sausages—but my mouth wouldn't form the words.

Veronica stuck her face in front of mine. Her eyes looked yellower than they usually did, but then,

Veronica and I didn't usually see eye to eye. "David," she said slowly, like she was talking to a dog (or a very small human being). "Have you ever broken a bone before?"

"I don't think so," I replied as my head flopped to the side. "Radcliff's our bone-breaker."

"Well, who said a family couldn't have more than one?" she asked as she unknotted her silk scarf and wadded it up in my hand. It felt like rain and smelled like watermelon. "Here, hold on to this. We need to keep pressure on the wound."

"You know, you probably shouldn't do that. Haven't you noticed that I'm…bleeding! Oh my crap, I'm really bleeding. Did you know that I'm bleeding? I think someone might have shot me." I scowled up at her. "Did *you* shoot me, Veronica?"

Instead of answering, she took her scarf back and stretched it tight, then paused. "I should probably warn you that this is going to hurt."

That was the last thing she said before I finally blacked out.

When I opened my eyes, I could tell immediately that I wasn't in my bed, that it was hours past morning. My mattress was slightly more comfortable than whatever I was lying on, and my mouth already tasted like stale Lucky Charms.

I groaned and rolled over. The bed squeaked like an exam table from a doctor's office. When I popped an eye open, I realized that it *was* an exam table from a doctor's office. And when I tried to sit up, I put my weight on my right hand and almost blacked out again.

Someone touched my arm. "You should probably take it easy. That door stripped those fingers to the bone—and probably broke them, too."

At the sound of *her* voice, the details came flooding back. I remembered Mr. Ashton, Mr. Lietz, the girls' bathroom, Veronica. I turned around, and there she was, as formidable as always in one of the office's plastic chairs.

Carefully, very carefully, I propped myself up. "I think you mean *you* broke them." The closet-sized room, which smelled like cherry suckers, slanted dangerously to one side.

She caught me when I fell. "Didn't I say to take it easy?" Her hair tickled my cheek as she lowered me back down to the table. "Apparently, you faint easily."

I eased my legs over the table and leaned back against the wall. Veronica hovered over me until she was sure that I was stable, then sat back down in her seat. It wasn't until I tried to rub my nose that I noticed the bandage.

"What's this?" I demanded, waving my right hand in her face.

Veronica lowered her gaze. "Nurse Schaefermeyer was afraid that your fingers might get infected, so she wrapped them up to keep them safe."

I waved it around like a white flag. "What am I supposed to do with it?" I asked. Then the truth dawned on me. "How am I supposed to *play*?"

The blood drained from her cheeks. "Does it really hurt that bad?"

"Well, I don't know," I said, scowling. "How bad do you think it would hurt to have the flesh stripped off your fingers?"

She didn't take the bait. "What about your other hand? You didn't hurt it, too, did you?"

"Sorry, *Ronny*," I replied, "but I can only play with one."

Her nostrils shriveled into slits. "You can call me lots of things, *Davy*, but I won't let you call me that."

Guilt rumbled in my stomach like a bowl of Mom's goulash. "All right," I said softly, but I'd crossed a line, and we both knew it. Under my breath, I added, "I'm sorry for calling you names."

Veronica sighed. "And I'm sorry for smashing your fingers."

We lapsed into an awkward silence, but for some reason, it wasn't as awkward as it probably should have been. Just outside the door, computers hummed, and voices chattered, but we just sat there listening, as still as a pair of stones. But it wasn't because we didn't know what to say to one another; it was because, for the first time, we didn't have to say anything.

When her foot started tapping, I immediately recognized the beat. "You're playing it, aren't you?"

Her foot went still. "What am I playing?"

I nodded at her feet. "You're playing the nocturne."

She set them flat on the floor. "I don't see why that's important."

I could have fired off a snappy comeback, but for some reason, I didn't want to. "Why do you get so defensive when anyone mentions the nocturne? I only told Mr. Lietz because I thought he'd want to hear it."

She didn't scowl, just sighed. "And a part of me wants him to hear it. But the rest of me just…"

"*What*?"

Veronica looked down at her toes. "Come on," she said. "You've met my parents. You know what they're like. If Dad found out that Mr. Lietz was going to be at the recital, he'd probably pop a string." Under her breath, she added, "And Mom would just ask for his number."

"So we won't tell them," I replied. Though I'd never been an evil mastermind, I couldn't help but get excited as a plan unfolded in my head. "We won't even tell Mr. Ashton."

"He already knows," she said. "You spilled in front of him, remember?"

I batted that away. "But he's never heard you play it. It can be our little secret."

She folded her arms across her waist. "I don't keep secrets with dorks."

I nodded. "Fair enough. But do you keep secrets with friends?"

NINETEEN

I SNUCK A PEEK AROUND the curtain, careful to stay out of sight. The spotlight was already on, so I couldn't see the audience, but I knew they could see me. And the last thing I wanted to do was let someone catch a glimpse of me before I absolutely had to.

My new shoes chafed, and my collar threatened to choke me. I'd worn plenty of ties over the years, but until Mom had bought me this new suit (my first), I'd made do with clip-ons. I couldn't draw a normal breath, and I was sweating like a drum major on the Fourth of July. I'd probably smell like gym shorts for a week—and I was nowhere near as nervous as Veronica appeared to be.

She was sitting in a nearby chair, her back straight and her shoulders square. If I hadn't gotten to know her as well as I had in these last couple of weeks, I would have thought that she was calm, but her slightly bulging eyes betrayed her. She was as freaked out as I'd ever seen her.

"It's all right if you're scared," I said, shoving my good hand into my pocket. "The truth is, I was terrified when I joined the race, but I think it's turned out all right. I mean, I'm only losing by, like, twenty points."

She almost cracked a smile. "Not your best pep talk, David."

"Sorry," I said, blushing. "I guess I don't have much experience."

She motioned toward the curtain. "Can you see where Mr. Lietz is sitting?"

He'd already stopped by to wish us luck, but we hadn't seen him since. I snuck another peek around the curtain, but the spotlight was too bright to make out more than dim outlines. I hoped Mr. Ashton hadn't stuck him too far back. The auditorium was just the lunchroom with the tables pushed out of the way and a curtain strung across the stage, so it had horrible acoustics.

Solemnly, I shook my head. "The spotlight's too bright," I replied. "They must have just replaced the bulbs."

She was too busy hyperventilating to appreciate my joke. "I shouldn't have let you talk me into this."

I could take Veronica's indifference and even her disdain, but I didn't know what to do with her apparent lack of confidence. I wanted to run away (or maybe offer her my pocket square so she could blow her nose), but Mr. Ashton turned the corner before I could make up my mind.

"How are my rising stars?" he asked.

We were too busy gaping at his outfit to come up with a response. His tight-fitting tuxedo was the color of a robin's egg, but it was his red cummerbund that completely captured my attention. He looked like the Devil's disco ball.

Mr. Ashton rubbed his jaw. "I guess I'll take that as fantastic."

I forced myself not to wince.

He motioned toward my bandaged hand. "Are you sure you'll be all right?"

I swallowed, hard. "Of course."

Those two fingers had been broken, so we'd been telling everyone that I was mostly ambidextrous. Mr. Ashton hadn't questioned it, but I was pretty sure Mom and Dad hadn't believed me. Luckily, they hadn't pressed me for details. If I was willing to participate, they were willing to go along with it. That was one of the perks of being the youngest of six boys.

Mr. Ashton clapped. "Well, then, let the show begin!"

He vanished as quickly as he'd come, and I released a held-in breath. My bandaged hand was aching, and if he'd stayed another second, I might have accidentally grimaced and given myself away. But if I was fading fast, Veronica looked like she was already gone.

"Are you okay?" I whispered.

At least that snapped her out of it. "Yeah," she said, "I am."

I drew a shaky breath. Even though my hand was aching and I felt like pulling down the curtain and using it to take a nap, I was more worried about Veronica. "You know," I said quietly, "we could just do 'La Vie en rose.' Or you could, anyway. I wouldn't be able to keep up, but your part would still sound great. Mr. Lietz would under—"

"No."

I bit my lip. "Okay."

Her shoulders drooped. "I'm sorry. I meant that *I* can't do it. I can't let them keep winning." One corner of her mouth curled up. "But I appreciate the offer."

I dipped my head. "Of course."

And that was how we settled it. But Mr. Ashton had positioned us at the end of the program (in "the sweet spot," as he'd called it), so we were still in for a wait. I tried to relax while the others played their pieces, but it was hard not to pay attention to their off-key groans and shrieks. They sounded just like a bunch of twelve-year-olds fumbling their way through the masters, but the audience still clapped and cheered like they were the New York Philharmonic. If that was their reaction to an off-key "Für Elise," they were going to go crazy when Veronica went on.

At some point during "The Stars and Stripes Forever," I sat down on the dusty floor and leaned back against the wall. Mr. Ashton hadn't made us play with the other members of the band, so we had a few more minutes off. I tried to close my eyes, but I was too wound up to rest. When Mr. Ashton took the stage again, I was wide awake.

"And now, ladies and gentlemen, for the moment you've been waiting for! I would introduce my stars, but I'm sure that their rendition of Edith Piaf's 'La Vie en rose' will introduce them for me." He waved us onto the stage. "I give you David Grainger and Veronica Pritchard-Pratt!"

The curtain muffled the applause, but it still nearly knocked me flat. If that was what it sounded like from all the way back here, then how was it going to sound from the middle of the stage? I struggled to my feet and took a quick swipe at my pants. They seemed to have a flair for attracting dust and lint.

I followed Veronica onto the stage. Her mouth was set in a grim line, but her steps were sure and confident. She looked like a class president slowly marching to her death. How had I ever thought that she couldn't do the job?

By the time we reached our instruments, I'd gone back to sweating. Despite the three-week campaign, I still hadn't gotten used to having every eye on me.

I pulled my mouthpiece from my pocket—it didn't feel right in my left hand—and slowly shined it on my sleeve. The silence was so perfect that you could hear my mouthpiece shriek as I slid it into its slot. I winced despite myself, then raised my trumpet to my lips. When I nodded at Veronica, she nodded back at me, and a peaceful, perfect stillness spread through my arms and legs. At least I didn't have to be up here alone.

I tapped out four beats so we could find our rhythm, and then she filled the silence with "La Vie en rose." I picked up on my line, just like I was supposed to, but we only stuck with Edith Piaf for another measure or two. After I bumbled through a fanfare that Veronica had come up with, she launched into a bridge to link "La Vie en rose" to the nocturne.

I hadn't heard her play it since that morning in the band room, but it was just as great as I remembered. It might have sounded happy if she'd played it faster, louder, but she played every note like she was pulling it up from her toes. Like it took everything she had to draw the music from her soul.

When she pushed through those thirty-second notes harder than she had before, I remembered I had a descant coming up. She'd thought I would look stupid if I just stood there breathing in the middle of the stage, so she'd dashed off this countermelody to give me something to do.

My fingers throbbed in time as I raised my trumpet to my lips, but adrenaline was coursing through me, so I barely registered the pain. And though my notes were flat and hollow compared to Veronica's round ones, they did provide a nice contrast to Frédéric Chopin's original. I'd always thought of music as a set of notes you had to play, but she clearly thought of music as a living, breathing thing—and she knew how to bring it to life.

While Veronica breezed through the rest, I took everything in. Dust motes swirled in the spotlight like fading specks of pixie dust, and anything seemed possible. I'd never believed in elves or fairies—I put my faith in the Justice League—but even I had to admit that this moment was magical. I really hoped her parents were out there somewhere, feeling the magic, too.

The nocturne should have been longer. It seemed like she'd just started when she reached the final chords. I blew my last fanfare, and then we both ended together. The notes hung in the air like hummingbirds, and for a moment, maybe more, everyone waited and wondered when those notes were going to scatter. But then the moment passed, and everyone jumped to their feet, clapping and catcalling and basically ignoring the rules that Mr. Ashton had provided on the back of the program.

I clapped and catcalled, too, but Veronica just sat there, stunned. I motioned for her to join me, but instead of basking in her applause, she hurried off the stage without even taking a bow.

TWENTY

I WENT AFTER HER, OF course, but by the time I reached the curtain, she'd already disappeared. I looked left, then right, but before I could decide which way to go, Mr. Ashton appeared out of nowhere.

"That was *stupendous*!" he announced, rattling the ceiling tiles. "You simply must do an encore!"

I shook my head. "We can't!"

"You can!" Mr. Ashton shouted.

"No, we can't!" I shouted back. "Veronica is gone."

He turned his ear toward me. "What did you say?" he replied.

"I said, Veronica is gone!" I gestured toward the flimsy curtain (which was shivering in the breeze). "So you're gonna have to tell them to stop clapping!"

The blood drained from his cheeks. "I can't say *that*!" he hissed.

"Well, you're gonna have to say something."

Mr. Ashton threw his arms up. "Fine!" After

straightening his lapels, he plastered a grin across his face and headed back onto the stage.

I should have known that Mr. Ashton could plaster grins across his face. I'd always thought of him as a late-night televangelist who'd missed his calling in life, but then, his real job wasn't much different.

While Mr. Ashton made our excuses, I dried my hand off on my pants. If I could figure out why she'd run off, I might be able to find her. But as soon as he made the announcement, people rushed onto the stage and poured around the flimsy curtain. Hands shook mine violently, and every time I turned around, someone wanted to say hi or compliment me on my performance. I wanted to grab them by the shoulders and tell them that it was Veronica, but no one would let me get a word in edgewise.

I was about to give up hope when I spotted a familiar bow tie on the outskirts of the crowd. "Mr. Lietz!" I shouted. "Hey, Mr. Lietz, over here!"

He couldn't see me right away, but when he spotted my bandaged hand (which I was waving frantically), he managed to work his way over. "Good evening, David," he replied. "What a magnificent performance—and with an injury, no less."

I batted that away. "I only had a few measures."

Mr. Lietz nodded knowingly. "And did you write the descant yourself?"

"Oh, no, that was Veronica. It was *all* Veronica."

Mr. Lietz clicked his heels together. "You two make quite the pair, don't you?"

I knew exactly what he meant. "You know, Mr. Lietz, she was really glad that you could come. She was just telling me that she thinks your school's pretty amazing."

Mr. Lietz smiled. "Then the feeling is mutual."

I didn't know what he meant by *that*, but I didn't have a chance to ask him before he cleared his throat.

"I'm afraid I have to go, but please tell Veronica that I'd be happy to discuss her options at her earliest convenience." He handed me a card (which I quickly stuffed in my back pocket), then gave my shoulder a pat. "I think you and Veronica have bright futures ahead."

I held up my hands. "Oh, no, I'm not interested…"

But I couldn't decide how to finish that sentence, so I didn't.

Mr. Lietz didn't press me. "You'll tell Veronica?" he asked.

I dipped my head. "Of course."

"Then I should let you get back to your celebration."

Mr. Lietz slipped away as silently as a ninja, leaving

me to navigate the backstage brawl alone. The crowd whirled and swirled around me, poking, prodding, jostling, but when I caught a whiff of lilac, I knew that I'd found Mom.

"David," she said softly, wrapping her arms around me from the side, "that was the loveliest thing I've ever heard. I think you and that trumpet are finally starting to get along."

"It wasn't me, it was Veronica." I took a step back so I could look Mom in the eyes. "You haven't seen her, have you?"

"No," Mom said, shaking her head. "Not since your performance, anyway."

I glanced over her shoulder. "I just need to tell her…"

"What?"

That the nocturne had been awesome. That she was smart and strong and brave. That Mr. Lietz wanted to discuss her options at her earliest convenience. But I couldn't bring myself to say those things out loud.

"Oh, nothing," I replied as I scratched the back of my head.

Mom smiled knowingly. "Then you'd better go and find her."

Dad, who'd been fending off the teeming hordes,

raised a hand to shield his eyes. "You'd think she'd be easy to spot."

I felt my shoulders slump. "She isn't here, is she?" I asked.

Dad clapped me on the back. "Then there's just one thing to do."

I crinkled my nose. "What's that?"

"Why, get out of here!" he said as he cleared a path toward the door.

I glanced at him, then at Mom, then plunged headfirst into the opening. For the first time since I'd broken them, my fingers didn't hurt at all.

The first thing I did when I burst into the hall was stop to catch my breath. The crowd was a lot thinner out here, so it wasn't as difficult to see. I checked both ways, then stopped to think, trying to decide which way to go. A few scattered clumps of people were milling around the commons, so I bet she'd headed south.

I found her outside the south door, just down the hall from the band room. She was talking with her parents, which I assumed was a good sign, since they clearly hadn't killed her. The recessed lights overhead dripped liquid gold onto their cheeks, softening their harsh features and blurring their rough edges.

It made Ms. Pritchard look more beautiful and Mr. Pratt look less severe.

I looped my arms across my chest and settled in to wait them out. I didn't mean to eavesdrop, but someone had propped the door open, so I couldn't help but overhear.

"—were amazing," Mr. Pratt was saying. My jaw nearly dropped.

Ms. Pritchard nodded her agreement as she puffed on her cigarette. I guess she hadn't noticed the NO SMOKING sign behind her. "Those folks would've followed you to the moon and back," she said. "That's power, Ronny. That's *real* power."

Veronica crinkled her nose. "I don't play for power, Mom, and I don't play for praise, either." She lowered her gaze. "I play to show people what I look like from the inside looking out."

Ms. Pritchard smirked. "Well, you certainly did *that*. You might as well have taken all your clothes off and run around naked on that stage."

I forced myself not to snort. Why did Ms. Pritchard ruin everything?

Mr. Pratt ignored her. "So why do you need Lietz House?"

"Yeah," Ms. Pritchard said, aiming her cigarette at Veronica. "Aren't we good enough for you?"

She opened her mouth to answer, then snapped it shut again. "No," she finally said, "you're not."

Ms. Pritchard's lips puckered. Mr. Pratt gritted his teeth. A part of me felt proud of her, but another part felt sad, too. If her parents weren't enough, then I wasn't enough, either, but then, that didn't surprise me. I'd already figured out that she was meant for bigger, better things.

"I want to *do* things," she went on. It was like she'd read my mind. "Learn a language, see the world." When she dropped her gaze this time, a shadow fell across her face. "I want to be more than what I am."

Ms. Pritchard stuck her hands on her hips. "What's wrong with being a Pritchard-Pratt?" she asked.

"*Nothing*," Veronica replied. "But what's wrong with being a better one?"

It was a legitimate question, but Mr. Pratt didn't take the time to answer it, just patted her arm.

"Well," he said diplomatically, "we don't have to decide tonight. You're, what, ten, eleven?"

She tossed her hair over her shoulder. "I'm twelve and a half," she said.

"When did *that* happen?" he asked, scratching the back of his head. When no one answered, he added, "You've become quite a young lady."

Veronica half snorted, half gurgled. When a tear spilled down her cheek, I realized that she was crying. Embarrassment squirmed in my stomach, but before I could decide whether I was supposed to go or stay, something amazing happened: Mr. Pratt grabbed his daughter's arm and pulled her into a hug.

They just stood there hugging for what felt like a long time, Mr. Pratt's sweat-stained T-shirt muffling her louder sobs. Ms. Pritchard puffed on her cigarette, seemingly unaffected by this display, but it was all that I could do not to gawk. Any leftover ideas that might have been shuffling around my head instantly melted away, and I was forced to accept that Veronica was a human being, with goods and bads and hopes and fears. We might not have had a lot in common, but in every way that mattered, we were exactly alike.

I'd just decided to leave when Veronica sniffled. I probably should have kept going, but like a moron, I looked back. As soon as our eyes met, I knew that I'd been caught white-handed.

I covered my face with my bandaged hand, furious at myself for staying. I thought about slinking away, but she'd already seen me. There was no reason to run now.

Mr. Pratt and Ms. Pritchard touched Veronica's arm, then went their separate ways. Ms. Pritchard swayed up the sidewalk, but Mr. Pratt headed back in. When he dipped his head at me, I blushed down to my toes.

I waited until her parents had vanished, then awkwardly shuffled out the door. The evening hadn't turned to night, so the sky was pink and frothy, like a strawberry milkshake. The doorway still smelled like smoke, but it smelled flowery, too, like Ms. Pritchard's perfume. For once, it didn't make me gag.

"I'm sorry," I said. "I really didn't mean to eavesdrop. I just had all these things to tell you, and when I found you, I just…stayed."

It was a pretty lame excuse, but she didn't call me on it, just tilted her head back and stared solemnly up at the sky.

"Anyway," I hurried on, "I just wanted to tell you that the nocturne sounded great. I mean, you sounded great. I mean, you sounded great while you were playing the nocturne."

She half smiled, half winced. "Yeah, my dad said the same thing."

"I know, I heard him," I replied, then realized how that must have sounded. "Not that I was trying to overhear him. It's just that someone left the door open, so I could hear what he was saying." I tugged at my bandage, accidentally unraveling a loose thread. "Oh, and Mr. Lietz wanted me to give you this."

I handed her the card (which had gotten slightly crumpled), but she didn't bother to inspect it, just tucked it into her pocket and blinked up at the sky. I had to force myself not to shake words out of her. When she was ready, she would talk. Until then, I'd have to wait. I shoved my good hand in my pocket, then carefully pulled it back out. Shoved it in, then pulled it out.

Finally, I blurted, "I think you should be class president."

Veronica didn't react. "Then I'm sure Spencer is glad that it isn't up to you."

I honestly couldn't decide whether or not she believed me. The milkshake sky faded to purple, then, finally, settled on blue. Even though it was the end of May, a cold wind whipped down the street, and I turned to go inside, but I didn't make it through the door before she said, "She gave it to me."

I glanced back. "Who gave you what?"

"My piano," she replied. "You asked me where I got it, and I told you that I stole it. But I didn't really steal it. Old Lady Foster gave it to me after Evelyn told her she didn't want it. When Evelyn found out, she threw this terrible fit and tried to convince her grandma to take it back. Luckily, her grandma didn't budge." She sent me a sideways glance. "I just wanted you to know."

I swallowed. "Thanks for telling me."

Veronica half nodded, half shrugged. "How would I have moved it, anyway?"

I blushed despite myself. "Well, I thought of that, but...never mind."

She perked up. "No, what'd you think?"

I fumbled for an answer that wouldn't make me sound idiotic, then, finally, settled on the truth: "That you were a superhero."

Veronica's sad smile didn't make it to her eyes. "I guess I'll see you tomorrow."

"Yeah," I said. "Tomorrow."

The election had always seemed so far away, and now it was just around the corner, only one wake-up away. I didn't think that I was ready—but ready or not, here it came.

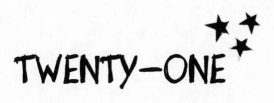

TWENTY-ONE

THE DÉJÀ VU MADE me jumpy. As I snuck a peek around the curtain, I couldn't help but dodge the spotlight (even though it wasn't on). If it hadn't been for my *Ghostbusters* shirt (circa 1993), I might have thought that I'd been sucked back into last night's recital.

At least it had occurred to them to leave a chair for me. It looked exactly like Veronica's, but I still couldn't sit down. I was as jittery as Ms. Clementi after her morning cup of coffee, but that was probably Spencer's fault.

"David!" he shouted in my face. Though it was barely after eight, his breath already smelled like Cheetos. "Are you even listening to me?"

"No, not really," I admitted. I was through with scams and lies.

He raked a hand through his black hair. He must have forgotten that he'd gelled it, because his hand came away sticky. "Well, concentrate!" he said, pointing his chin at my shirt. "If I didn't know better, I'd think you weren't taking this seriously."

Not only had he done his hair, but he'd borrowed a suit for the occasion. He'd wanted me to dress up, too, but I was also through with suits.

"Listen," Spencer whispered after glancing at Veronica, "I took the last straw poll this morning. As long as you don't mess this up, I'm sure we've got it in the bag."

I wrinkled my nose. His Cheeto breath was overwhelming. Maybe he ate them for breakfast, or maybe he ate them in his sleep. For some reason, that thought made me giggle uncontrollably.

Spencer shook my shoulders. "What are you laughing at?" he asked. "It's like aliens sucked out your brain."

I gave him a not-so-playful shove. "My brain's right here, all right? So you can stop hyperventilating." I tried not to smack him as I straightened my shirt. "It's not like I'm running for Supreme Dictator of the Galaxy."

Spencer fixed his tie. "You're right. You're running for class president, which is actually, you know, *real*."

I forced myself to keep my mouth shut. He was perfectly entitled to his own stupid opinions.

Once Spencer could tell that I wasn't going to disagree with him, he jerked some cards out of his pocket. "Your speech," he said sharply as he handed them to me.

I thumbed through the cards while Spencer paced back and forth. This speech was more Riley's than mine, since he was the one who'd written it. It was called "Your Voice, Your Vote," and though it was a wonder of modern speechwriting and we'd spent the last few days going over it, I couldn't recall a single word. Also, my vision was so blurry that his handwriting looked like Japanese.

I was still reviewing Riley's cards—or at least *trying* to review them—when Ms. Quintero made her entrance. Anxiety growled in my stomach as her heels clicked to a halt. When Veronica looked up, I tried to get her attention, but she was so fixed on Ms. Quintero that she didn't notice me.

Ms. Quintero set her sights on Spencer. "You may take your seat now, Mr. Chen. Your candidate is on his own from here."

He smacked my back one more time, then headed for his front-row seat. Just before he disappeared, he leveled a finger at me. "Don't mess this up, or I *will* kill you."

I didn't bother to reply.

Ms. Quintero cleared her throat. "I'm sure I don't need to remind you that I expect no tricks, no funny business. You will sit where I tell you to sit, and you will talk when I tell you to talk. You will not drool or pick your nose, and you certainly won't make a scene." She gave me the hairy eyeball. "Have I made myself clear?"

My mouth was too dry to form words, but I did manage to nod.

"Very well," Ms. Quintero said. "If you'll please follow me."

I swallowed, hard, then followed Veronica onto the stage. The risers from last night had mysteriously vanished, so except for two plastic chairs and the scuffed-up podium (which was older than I was), the stage was deserted. It looked even more threatening than it had last night.

Ms. Quintero marched up to the podium, and the audience quieted down. "Welcome to this morning's assembly. As you know, you'll soon be voting for the boy or girl you want to represent you as next year's class president. The candidates, David Grainger and Veronica Pritchard-Pratt, will have one last chance to win your votes with their remarks this morning. We'll begin with our incumbent." Ms. Quintero glanced at Veronica. "Ms. Pritchard-Pratt, you have the floor."

Veronica leaped out of her seat, much more confident than she'd been the night before. She'd traded in her usual All Stars for a pair of bright-red heels, and her knee-length skirt, plain black, looked positively presidential.

I was the only one who knew that she'd bought them secondhand.

"Good morning, Shepherd's Vale!" she said, then paused so they could whoop and holler. "It's an honor to be here this morning. I guess I have my opponent, the distinguished David Grainger, to thank for this opportunity."

When she saluted me, I forced myself not to wince. I'd gotten into this race because I hadn't believed—in Veronica *or* myself—and now my plan was backfiring.

"There's been a lot of talk about ideas over the course of this campaign, and my opponent's had some great ones. Those mirrors were amazing, and I know I wasn't the only one who wanted one of those shirts."

Someone whistled something that I didn't recognize, which made Veronica smile, which made everyone else laugh. It was a good moment for her. I snuck a peek at Esther, the *real* source of our ideas, and she was grinning from ear to ear. I'd probably just lost a vote, but strangely, I didn't care.

That thought was still rattling around my brain when Veronica gripped the podium with both hands. "But this race isn't about T-shirts or even great ideas. It's about picking the right person at the right time, and I'm here to tell you that the right person is *me*."

Veronica had leaned in for this part, and the audience had leaned in, too. Her voice wasn't as hypnotic as her piano, but it was awfully close.

"Now, I could tell you," she went on, "that I'm going to cancel seventh period and return pop to the vending machines, but I'm not going to do that. I could tell you that I'm going to extend Christmas vacation and cut the rest of the year in half, but I'm not going to do that, either. No class president has that kind of power, and no class president ever will."

I tugged at my bandage. Where was she going with this speech?

"Which brings me," she continued, "to my most important question—why *do* I think that you should vote for me instead of my distinguished opponent? If we don't have any real power, then why does it even matter?"

She let that question dangle for what seemed like

an eternity, until everyone in every seat was waiting breathlessly for her reply.

"It matters," she finally whispered, "because I want this more than he does. Because I *need* this more than he does." She finally leaned back. "I always have, I always will."

I was probably the only person who'd caught those last couple of words, but no one seemed to notice. Veronica had just delivered one whopper of a speech, so everyone was satisfied—everyone except for me. They might have thought it was an act, but I knew it was real.

"Thank you," Veronica added, and the audience exploded. Why had I thought this place had bad acoustics? The catcalls were loud enough to shatter my eardrums.

Veronica paid them no heed as she went back to her seat. Our shoulders brushed as she sat down, sending a jolt of electricity down my spine. What was I going to say *now*? I snuck a peek at Spencer, hoping he'd know what to do, but he just shook his head and mouthed, *I think we've got this in the bag.* Or maybe he'd mouthed, *If you ruin this, you're dead.* Either way, he hadn't helped.

I knew I had to get up and give my speech, but it felt

like I was weighed down with thick chains. I was the only one who knew Veronica's truth, so I was the only one who could decide what I was supposed to do with it.

But I couldn't make up my mind.

Ms. Quintero stirred. "Mr. Grainger?"

At least that snapped me out of it. I squeezed Riley's cards and dragged myself out of my seat. The short walk to the podium felt more like a marathon. I was nearly there when I tripped over a cord and hog-tied the podium. The microphone shrieked in protest as I struggled to regain my balance.

"Hello!" I finally blurted, and the microphone shrieked again. I put down Riley's cards, which were now crumpled and useless, and tried to clear my throat. "I mean, thank you for letting me get up here and talk to you today."

The spotlight wasn't on, so I could see the audience, and they could see me. When I spotted Spencer, I couldn't hold his gaze. It was almost like he knew I was about to mess this up, but there was nothing he could do.

When I looked back down, my eyes landed on the wad of crumpled cards, and my fear turned into guilt. Riley had poured everything he had into that speech. It certainly deserved to be given.

But I couldn't bring myself to do it.

I nudged the cards out of the way and gripped the podium with my good hand. "You probably think I joined this race because I didn't think Veronica should be our class president." If she could come clean, then I could, too. "But that's only part of it. The truth is, I joined this race because I opened my big mouth and couldn't find a way to say, 'I'm sorry.' And because the MMM accidentally poked me in the eye."

The audience blinked and looked around. Thankfully, the MMM, who'd just poked her head through the side door, didn't seem to know who I was talking about.

"I've learned a lot lately," I said, "and the most important thing I've learned is that people can surprise you. Sometimes they look different on the inside than they do on the out, and sometimes you discover you have a lot more in common than you ever thought you could."

I drew a ragged breath. If I didn't say it now, I didn't think I ever would, and if I never found a way to say it, Veronica probably wouldn't win. And if she didn't win this race, it might throw off the delicate balance of music and the universe. What if it broke her will to win? What if she didn't get into Lietz House?

And what if I just thought she'd make a better class president?

I drew a bracing breath and prayed that Spencer would forgive me. "So don't vote for me. Vote for Veronica Pritchard-Pratt."

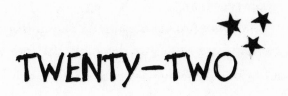

TWENTY-TWO

IT ONLY TOOK A second for pandemonium to break out. Everyone burst to their feet—everyone except for Spencer. His face had flushed purple, and it looked like he was shouting, but the clapping was so loud that I couldn't tell what he was saying. That was probably a good thing.

I just stood there, dazed. Why was everyone freaking out? This hadn't been part of the plan. I guess it was possible that they'd misunderstood.

"Vote for Veronica!" I said again, and the audience pumped their fists. But before I could pump mine, Ms. Quintero grabbed my elbow and steered me back to my seat. I didn't realize that my bandage had snagged on a corner of the podium until three feet of gauze had unraveled behind me. While I scrambled to rewind it, the audience cheered.

Ms. Quintero held her hands up. "That's enough!" she said firmly, and everyone sat back down. "We'd like to thank Mr. Grainger and Ms. Pritchard-Pratt for their stirring remarks and dismiss for second period. The bell will ring in four minutes and twelve seconds, so I suggest you get to class."

The audience hopped back up and calmly filed out of the room. Ms. Quintero picked up Riley's speech and carefully smoothed it back out. I couldn't see her face, but I doubted it would have told me anything. Rumor had it that Ms. Quintero was an underground poker player, but I put less stock in rumors these days.

"Your speech," she said calmly as she handed it to me. "Or your old speech, anyway."

I felt my cheeks redden. "Thanks," I mumbled lamely, shoving the cards into my pocket.

"Well played," Ms. Quintero said with a respectful tip of her head. "I can honestly say I didn't think you had it in you, but I guess you've changed my mind."

Ms. Quintero's heels clicked away before I had a chance to ask her what she meant, so I asked Veronica instead: "What do you think she meant by that?"

Veronica just shook her head. "If you're fishing for a compliment, I'm not going to bite."

I felt my pulse speed up. "But I told them to vote for you."

"*Exactly*," she replied. "You've built your whole

campaign on clever jokes and cool one-liners, and as far as jokes go, that was one of the best."

"But it wasn't a joke!" I wanted to tear my hair out. "Honestly, Veronica, I meant every word."

She tilted her head to the side. "You know, I think I believe you." With a sad smile, she added, "I guess it's too bad that they don't know you as well as I do."

I spent the rest of second period trying to convince the other BGs that I'd meant what I'd said, but none of them believed me. They thought it was all a joke, and Veronica didn't set the record straight.

Third period was no better, and fourth period couldn't have gone worse. By the time lunch rolled around, I felt like a powder keg with a millimeter-long fuse, so when Spencer showed up with a huge smirk on his face, I almost lost it on the spot.

"This is all *your* fault," I growled, resisting the urge to lunge for him.

"No," Spencer said, grinning, "I'm pretty sure it's yours. That speech was brilliant, by the way."

Esther nodded glumly. "Not that I want to agree with Spencer, but I think he might be right."

"Then we've got to tell them," I replied. "We've got to *make* them understand."

Spencer shook his head. "No, you've already done

that. Now we just have to sit back and let destiny run its course."

I'd never been a fan of destiny, and now I realized why.

When the seventh-grade student council showed up during fifth period to pass around the ballots, I made a show of circling Veronica's name, but everyone assumed that I was still messing around. That I was going to erase it and circle DAVID GRAINGER instead. I never erased it, but no one seemed to care.

On my way out of class, Ms. Park discreetly pulled me aside. "It was awfully sporting of you to vote for Veronica," she said.

I fought the urge to smack my forehead.

✳ ✳ ✳

I won the election in the most lopsided victory that SV had ever seen. They announced the results before the bell rang. The other kids exploded, but I didn't join in. I was too busy wondering where Veronica was and how she'd reacted to the news.

The halls turned into a carnival as soon as the bell rang. I ducked into the bathroom to ride out the worst of it. By the time I dared to poke my head out, the partygoers had moved on. Blue silly string covered the walls, and homemade confetti littered the ground. I knew it was homemade because none of the pieces looked the same. Though I felt bad for the janitors (and for beating Veronica), I couldn't help but feel grateful for Esther, who must have stayed up all night cutting, banking on the fact that I would win.

I stopped at my locker, which was plastered with well wishes (including Spencer's proud "Take THAT!" and Esther's quick-thinking heads-up that they were headed to Renfro's), then headed down to the band room. A month ago, I wouldn't have thought twice about abandoning my trumpet, but now I couldn't imagine going anywhere without it.

When I got to the commons, it didn't surprise me to discover that Veronica's banner had been torn down and cleanly severed at the neck. I guess it was a good thing that they'd had the banner to decapitate. I shuddered to think what would have happened if I'd been the one who'd lost.

I was halfway down the hall when the nocturne reached my ears. What started as a jog quickly morphed into a sprint, and before I knew it, I was barreling into Mr. Ashton's room.

"I meant—it," I half said, half gasped. "What I said in—my speech."

She didn't look up from the keys. "You already said that," she replied.

I drew a noisy breath. "*I* voted for you," I told her before I thought better of it.

One corner of her mouth curled up, but she didn't stop playing. "Then at least I got one vote."

I looked down at my toes. How had I gotten this so *wrong*?

"You know," she finally said, "it really isn't that awful."

"What isn't that awful?" I replied.

"The job," she said, still playing. "In fact, I think you're going to do great."

I collapsed into a nearby chair. "And I think I'm gonna do terrible."

Veronica cocked an eyebrow. "Why would you think that?" she asked.

"Because I can't read people," I said. "Take Hector, for example."

She tilted her head to the side. "He *is* a bully," she replied.

"Because he grew up on the streets!" I plopped my chin into my hands. "Why didn't I know where he came from?"

Instead of answering, she shrugged. "Why did I think you'd be a pushover?"

That caught me off guard. "Did you really think I'd go down easily?"

"Of course," Veronica replied. "It wasn't like I wanted to lose."

"Then why'd you challenge me?" I asked. "And why didn't you let Ms. Quintero kick me out?"

Veronica played the nocturne's final chord, then gently closed the piano lid. "I already told you," she replied, hoisting her bag over her shoulder. "I was sick of winning by default." She sent me a sideways glance. "And by the time that you and Esther came up with those awesome shirts, a part of me was rooting for you, too."

I expected her to leave, but she just stood there waiting. She'd taken off her heels—I could see them poking out of her bag—so she was back to being tall, not completely gargantuan. It made her look less imposing (or maybe she just didn't scare me anymore).

"You know," she finally said, "I should probably thank you."

"For *what?*" I asked, snorting.

"For everything," she said. "But mostly for last night." She dug her toe into a crack. "I don't think

I could have told them what we showed them with that piece."

"What *you* showed them," I replied. "I was just the background noise."

"Maybe," she admitted, which made me almost grin. "But I never would have done it if you hadn't forced me into it."

I held up my bandaged hand. "I did break my fingers for you."

"Actually," she said, "I'm pretty sure that *I* did that."

I made a show of shrugging. "Mr. Lietz said we make quite a team."

"You know, he may be on to something."

She grinned at me, and I grinned back. It was nice to know I had her in my corner—and I wanted to keep it that way.

"I want you to be my vice," I blurted.

Her eyes widened momentarily, but then she saluted. "Whatever you say, Mr. President." More seriously, she added, "Thanks."

I felt my cheeks get hot. "Also, I've been thinking...about integrating student council."

Veronica made a face. "So you *did* overhear," she said.

I nodded ruefully. "I guess I'm kind of good at that."

She looked down at her toes. "Well, it was only an

idea, and everyone thought it was a dumb one, so I decided to take it off—"

"I didn't."

"You didn't *what*?" she asked.

"Think it was stupid," I replied.

Veronica lowered her gaze. "Oh."

"Correct me if I'm wrong, but there are five student council seats, aren't there?"

Now it was her turn to nod.

"So what if we split them in half?"

"You can't split five seats in half," she said.

"So what if I take three seats and you take the other two? I'd give you the extra seat, but Spencer would probably have a fit."

Veronica smiled slyly. "They're your seats, Mr. President. That means you get to fill them with whoever you want."

I wrinkled my nose. "But what if I don't *want* to decide? Should I pick Hector and Samantha, or Samantha and Brady, or Brady and Hector?"

Veronica waved that off. "I'm sure you'll figure it out." She snaked her right arm through my left and practically hauled me out the door. "It's really not that difficult."

"How can *that* be?" I replied as I struggled to keep up.

"Because it's middle school," she said. "You come back and talk to me once they pick you to run the country."

I pretended to clutch my chest. "President of the United States? I don't think I could handle that."

"And I don't think you know what you could handle."

That thought made me miss a step, which made Veronica laugh. Maybe she was right. Maybe it was only a matter of time.

But I sincerely hoped not.

ACKNOWLEDGMENTS

First, thank you to Kate Testerman, who managed to sell three books for me in as many months after a year of discouragement. I'm glad you patted me on the head and told me to run along when I suggested that we quit.

Second, thank you to Steve Geck, who saw the potential in these band geeks and populars. I'm glad you think I'm funny. Also, thanks to everyone at Sourcebooks, especially Kate Prosswimmer, Elizabeth Boyer, and Alex Yeadon, and to John Aardema, Will Riley, and Chris Cocozza for the super fun cover.

My critique partners—Amy Sonnichsen, Ben Spendlove, Jenilyn Collings, Kelly Kennedy Bryson, Liesl Shurtliff, and Myrna Foster—are not just great writers but great people, and I can't thank them enough. This book probably would have ended up at the bottom of a cliff if it hadn't been for your encouragement, so I'm glad you talked me down.

Thank you to my parents, who now know far more about the publishing industry than they probably ever wanted to. I've always appreciated your unwavering support. Also, thanks to Heather and Adam Musser, my favorite sister and brother-in-law (on this side of the family), for humoring me when I asked them to teach me how to play a trumpet.

And of course, thank you to Chris, my sun, and to Isaac, Madeleine, and William, my bright, shining stars. I can't wait to watch you grow up and see what people you become.

ABOUT THE AUTHOR

Krista Van Dolzer is a stay-at-home mom by day and a children's author by bedtime. Though she's short like David, she plays the piano like Veronica. She also enjoys watching college football and researching her ancestors. Krista lives with her husband and three kids in Mesquite, Nevada.